RESTRAINED Desires

KATHERINE MCINTYRE

HOT TREE PUBLISHING

RESTRAINED DESIRES

REHOBOTH PACT BOOK THREE

KATHERINE MCINTYRE

HOT TREE PUBLISHING

For information, contact the publisher, Hot Tree Publishing.

www.hottreepublishing.com

Editing: Hot Tree Editing

Cover Designer: BookSmith Design

E-book ISBN: 978-1-922679-10-9

Paperback ISBN: 978-1-922679-11-6

ALSO BY KATHERINE MCINTYRE

REHOBOTH PACT

CONFINED DESIRES

OPPOSED DESIRES

RESTRAINED DESIRES

CHESAPEAKE DAYS

STRONGER THAN HOPE

STRONGER THAN PASSION

STRONGER THAN LONGING

OUTLAWS

MIDNIGHT HEIST

TWILIGHT HEIST

To those with the courage to find themselves.

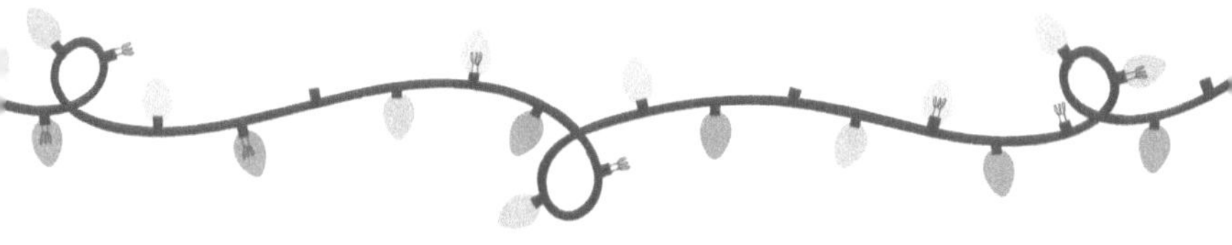

CHAPTER ONE

When it came to love, Kyle Walker fell in last place, every time.

Which should've made her feel better about the den of debauchery she'd be walking into tonight, especially since the event was orchestrated by her best friend Aubs. The no-holds-barred celebration of love's destruction was all in honor of Aubrey Moore's little sister and the brand-new divorce she filed.

Kyle tightened her grip on the chilly steering wheel, trying to summon the courage to get out of the car. Considering she remained staunchly camp dreamer in her search for the ever-elusive "one," this wasn't her cup of Tetley. And given the rest of the gang's recent coupling up, between Sky and Mia as well as Selina and Aubrey, she was the uncomfortable fifth wheel every time they all got together. She checked her smudged black eyeliner, which was the minimal makeup she wore tonight, in the rearview mirror.

Time to go celebrate with the rest of the gang and Chelsea Moore, a woman too hot to be real. Kyle prepared herself for the five million times Aubrey or Sky would nudge her in the side and try to get her to go and bat her lashes at anyone looking single and sultry at the bar. Last time she tried that move, the woman she was attempting to impress thought a bug had flown into her eye.

Right. She could do this. She popped the car door open and slipped out, bracing herself against the crisp bite of November breezes swirling around. Kyle hunched, digging her bare hands deep into the pockets of her canvas jacket.

The brick front of Vaudeville Emporium was located a few blocks up. It was the sort of bright, racy bar that drew out everyone from hippies to kinksters. Kyle had been shocked to hear not only were they going somewhere other than Renegades tonight, but they were also stepping out into her territory, Philly. In fact, Luxe Salon and Spa, where she massaged the wealthy and weird, lay a few blocks from here. Even better, her apartment was three blocks in the other direction.

The closer she got to Vaudeville, the more the pulsing music drifted from inside the bar. Kyle could feel the beats reverberating through her. She should try to meet someone tonight. After all, she'd made a massive mistake last week—one requiring a fast solution.

One she needed to put off for another day, at least.

She caught sight of a few folks wearing canvas jackets with activist patches all over them standing outside the bar and catching a smoke, and there was one goth outlier as well. Kyle made a beeline for the goth-chic owner of Renegades bar in Wilmington, Aubrey's girlfriend, Selina. The moment Selina caught sight of her, she flicked the stub of her cigarette to the ground and crushed it under her heavy heel. The woman was dressed all in black with striped leggings and a slouchy tunic accented by chunky silver jewelry. With the flick of her wrist, she gestured Kyle to follow.

"About time you showed up," she called out. "Aubrey was worried you bailed."

Kyle shook her head, striding in after Selina crooked the door open. "And miss the carnage that's sure to erupt with Chelsea Moore on the market again? Couldn't pass this up."

The scent of cigar smoke, hardwood, and plum filtered through the air, an odd blend of incense as they wafted through the place. Vaudeville Emporium featured a red backlit bar in the center of the place with cozy mahogany booths and carmine lampshades all around the perimeter. The framed pictures on the wall formed a menagerie of vintage pinup and Greek mythology, a combination she'd never quite figured out, but they fit with the mismatched chairs lining the bar and the odd bronze steampunk sculptures stationed throughout.

Kyle strode in time with Selina, casting her a wayward glance. "Has Aubs corralled a harem of eligible men for Chels yet? I'm hoping that'll take the pressure off me for the night."

Selina snorted. "You and I both know she comes on strong. Unfortunately for you, Chelsea seems to have no problem flirting and charming most of the room on her own, so Aubrey's going to be relentless in her quest to fix you up with the perfect someone."

"Then I need a fucking drink," Kyle murmured,

running a hand through her hair and messing up any effort she'd taken to style the ear-length locks. "Where are you all situated at?"

Selina tilted her head toward the back of the bar near the mini stage setup. A woman clad in belly-dance garb was performing a sexy burlesque number, strutting her stuff on the platform. Purple silks swished with her every movement. The corner booth on the far side contained plenty of familiar faces along with a few new ones. She hoped she didn't have to make small talk with the folks she didn't know because she failed abysmally at it every time.

Apparently, getting-to-know-you questions didn't include if they had any near-death experiences or believed in ghosts. Those were a drop in the pool of her myriad of terrible conversation starters that followed with one-word responses or folks making a quick getaway. She liked when she didn't have to bother with the nonsense and could be odd and direct around her friends without worrying if they viewed her like a total psycho.

Kyle sauntered to the bar lit with neon reds and ordered a gin and tonic, her standby. Maybe she clung to the usual too much, which stacked on top of the many reasons she hadn't found herself a steady relationship for years. She liked her same haircut, her job she'd worked at for the past decade, and the drink choice that never let her down, unlike the dozens of Tinder dates she'd been on.

The sultry song broadcast over the speakers, and a few folks in the crowd let out hoots and hollers as the dancer shed her slinky top first and her billowing skirt next. Kyle held back a shudder at the idea of standing up there exposed, stripped down to a performance bra and shorts that might as well be underwear. She could never—not with her stocky shoulders, her flat chest, and her bigger hips that hadn't taken the memo to flow with the rest of her body.

The bartender handed her a crisp gin and tonic, and she took the first sip to soothe her nerves before she headed to the back where everyone else waited. The burlesque performance came to a close to a bunch of riotous applause and some wolf whistles from the corner booth she was fast approaching. She shook her head, unable to hide her grin.

The dancer strode to the microphone. "We'll be playing the music over the next hour, and we welcome any amateurs who want to get up on stage and strut their stuff."

Kyle's stomach performed an acrobatic roll at the

thought. A resounding fuck no. The last thing she needed was crickets and disgusted stares as she humiliated herself publicly. The condensation of her glass met her sweaty palms as she closed the distance to the booth and prayed they wouldn't pluck members from the audience at random. She was standing a few feet away from the booth when she spotted Chelsea getting up from her seat.

Kyle allowed herself to linger on the sight of her, just a little bit. The woman wore her rich ash-brown hair in sultry waves, and crimson looked like sin on those lips that framed a perfect set of white teeth when she smiled. She brimmed with sex appeal in her apple-red top and the mid-thigh black skirt she wore with fishnets. Chelsea Moore had always been all sorts of off-limits—straight, married, and Aubrey's sister—but Kyle found it hard to look the other way when so much eye candy strutted in front of her.

In fact, the eye candy was strutting herself right to the stage. Oh God.

Kyle sank into the first open seat at the booth, thankfully next to Mia. "What did I miss?" she asked, placing her drink on the table in front of her.

"Woman of the night has decided to give burlesque a try. Aubrey's attempting to be encouraging while hiding her eyes." Mia grinned, tilting her head in Aubs's direction. Selina sat behind Aubrey, placing her hands over her girlfriend's eyes to hide the visual of her little sister flaunting her frustrations onstage.

"How does anyone find the stones to do that?" Kyle asked, shaking her head in disbelief. "I'd die."

Mia shrugged. "I don't know. It sounds like fun to me."

Kyle cast her a glance. "Yeah, but you're you. I'm.... No one wants to see this."

Mia bumped her shoulder against Kyle's. "Excuse me? None of the self-deprecating shit, Kyle Walker. You're ridiculously pretty."

A flush rose to her cheeks. She wished she didn't feel a wave of discomfort any time she got a compliment, like she'd gotten stood up on a date or got dragged out to play a softball game. They were hard to accept when she couldn't fight the chorus of criticisms barraging her daily, most of which she heard spoken in her mother's voice.

Kyle settled into the seat, her gaze returning to the stage where Chelsea stood waiting for the song to kick in. At least now Kyle had an excuse for gawking like a weirdo at the gorgeous woman. The shadows and lights onstage highlighted Chelsea's strong jaw, her defined brows, and her elegant nose. A seductive

1920s siren song trumpeted over the speakers, and Chelsea began to move.

"Is anything happening?" Aubrey called out.

"You'd know if you weren't being a prude," Sky shouted. Kyle's other best friend leaned back in the seat, still wearing her striped pants from working in the kitchen earlier, though she'd ditched the chef's jacket.

Kyle snorted and took another sip of her gin and tonic, fixated on the stage. Chelsea's smoky gaze roamed through the crowd as she began to slink and strut along the platform. She moved with a liquid command of her form, though it wasn't like she needed added confidence with a body that stunning. The woman was all hourglass curves, long tanned legs, and smooth bronze skin. Each coy movement she made was pure seduction, from the cock of her hips to her lips, as she followed in time to the music.

Chelsea's gaze landed on hers, and she forgot how to breathe. Kyle could only offer a weak smile as the woman levelled a frag grenade of sexuality in her direction. Like she needed more masturbation fodder. Chelsea's eyes remained on her while she dropped to the ground, thrusting her ass back as she rose again. She reached for the hem of her crimson shirt, teasing the fabric up her toned stomach, and a bunch of whistles pierced the room.

"This was a terrible plan," Aubrey called out from her seat.

"You only have yourself to blame, sunshine," Selina reminded her.

Chelsea quirked her lips into a knowing grin as she slipped the sides of her flimsy black skirt higher and higher along those perfect thighs Kyle would kill to bury herself between. Goddamn, this woman was a pure fantasy—and now recently divorced.

Straight. Chelsea Moore was straight, which meant she'd forever be that—a fantasy.

Chelsea whipped her sultry strands around as she flipped her skirt up, revealing black lace panties —not helping. The song kicked into a crescendo, those lusty vocals matching the provocative moves this woman kept upping. If Chelsea full-out stripped on stage, Aubrey would probably burn this place to the ground. Though Selina was right. Both of the Moore girls were sticks of dynamite, and this divorce had lit Chelsea right up.

Guys in the next booth over whistled louder than ever, nearly hanging out of it with their jaws dropped. Kyle couldn't blame them—the woman had become an inferno that made her want to burn to ash. Chelsea swung her hips, sliding her palms up her waist. She peeled the hem of her top up the whole way, revealing a matching black lace bra, which cupped her perky tits. She flicked the shirt up and off, twirling the fabric around her finger. The cheers grew even louder. Kyle's throat dried, and she took another absentminded sip of her gin and tonic, unable to look away.

Chelsea's gaze locked on hers again, and everything else in the room vanished, from the wildly hollering guys and girls around them to the scuff of shoes and clink of glasses by the bar. All she could focus on was the woman before her and the hypnotic way she moved. With those seductive eyes on hers, Kyle couldn't look anywhere else if she tried. The song reached a crescendo and was nearing the end as Chelsea pivoted around to bend over. Whistles pierced the air when she rolled back up, sliding her palms along those long, long legs made even sexier by her fishnets.

Chelsea finished by bringing the hem of her skirt up with the motion, exposing a perfect fucking ass encased in lace.

Kyle's head was dizzied from how turned on she was right now. Even though she knew Chelsea hadn't been looking her way—she'd been staring at their crew, obviously—the amount of eye contact from someone so damn pretty made her delirious.

She needed to be drunker to handle the rest of the evening.

The song came to a close, and their table erupted in screams. Kyle clapped, feeling like an idiot with the automatic motion that was so flimsy compared to the detonation of lust inside her. She couldn't force words from her mouth after watching a performance like that. Chelsea swept her arm in an extravagant bow and then strolled off stage, sliding her shirt over her head again.

"You can open your eyes now, Aubs," Chelsea called from feet away, her voice rich and a bit breathless, like she'd tried cliff diving for the first time. Honestly, Kyle would take cliff diving over performing on a stage, and heights terrified her. A lot of things terrified her, from her fear of needles to an inexplicable uneasiness around taxi drivers.

Selina removed her hands from Aubrey's eyes with a smirk, and Aubrey shook her head.

"Come on now, I love you, but I don't need to see my little sister strip onstage. That's just weird," Aubrey said in protest. One of Chelsea's friends leaned in toward Aubrey and must've whispered what had happened, because Aubs's features contorted a few different ways before settling on mock horror. "Hey, I'm supposed to be the deviant one, not you."

Chels snorted and swung over to where Kyle sat. "Gone for five minutes and already my spot's been stolen. About time you got here, Walker."

Kyle chewed on her lip, embarrassment flushing through her. "Crap, I'm sorry. I can find somewhere else...."

Chelsea's laugh rolled over her like honey as her eyes softened. "Relax. Just scooch in a little."

"Right. Can do," Kyle squeezed in closer to Mia who was leaning on Sky. "I mean, alternatively, I can stand. I've been told I'm really good at awkward looming."

Chelsea lifted a brow. "Keep your ass in that seat. I don't mind sharing space." Chelsea plopped down beside her, their thighs brushing from the proximity. This close, Kyle could see the light sheen of sweat on Chelsea's skin, and she caught the almond-and-leather scent of her perfume, which was absolutely mouthwatering. Fuck, Kyle buzzed with how hot this woman made her, and she was nervous Chels would look at her and suss out all these rampant pheromones.

"So, enjoying the celebration of your emancipation?" Kyle asked, attempting to do the thing she hated most—small talk. She took another tiny swig of gin and tonic, hoping the drink would cool her down. "Looks like you've managed to attract the attention of half the room, so you'll be drowning in guys in no time."

"The dark side of 'It's Raining Men,'" Chels murmured, snagging her bottle of beer and taking a swig. She pursed her lips, her gaze going distant for only a second—fast enough Kyle almost missed it. "If I wanted a drooling frat guy, I would've stayed with my husband."

Kyle's grip on her drink tightened, and the impulse had her opening her mouth before she could help herself. "I'm not going to ask if you're okay, because I'm sure you're sick of hearing that. But if you need a breather, or if you need to talk, I'm here."

Chelsea's lips quirked for a moment, and the woman's intense stare rolled over her like a crack of lightning. Kyle swallowed hard.

Chelsea nudged her thigh against Kyle's. "You're too damn sweet to be my sister's best friend. I bet the women who eat you out get a toothache."

Kyle spluttered mid-sip, almost spraying the liquid all over the table. Her cheeks flushed, the heat spreading through her whole body in seconds. She didn't even know how to respond, so she ducked her head and knifed her fingers through her hair. "Candysnatch would be a horrible nickname, just saying. No wonder I'm in such an epic dry spell."

"All the more reason to get loaded with me tonight," Chelsea said, lifting her bottle to clink it against Kyle's glass. "You've got some catching up to do."

"Guess my car's remaining parked out front." Kyle grinned. "Might as well reap the benefits of living three blocks away."

"What? You've been holding out, Walker," Chelsea declared before she tilted back her bottle and chugged the rest of her beer. "That's it. If I get stumble-drunk tonight, I'm crashing at your place."

Right, like that was a great idea. Having Chelsea sit right next to her, single, too gorgeous for words, and exuding enough confidence to slay a room affected Kyle enough, but having this powder keg of a woman in her apartment? Fuck, she'd combust on the spot.

Instead, her mouth did the talking for her. "You know you're always welcome over," she said, regretting those words the moment they passed her lips.

Chelsea's eyes lit up, and she pounded a fist to the table. "Time for another round. Who's with me?"

Aubs gave a hoot from the other side of the booth, and Sky stood up from her seat holding her and Mia's empties.

Kyle slurped down the rest of her gin and tonic.

Let the bad decisions begin.

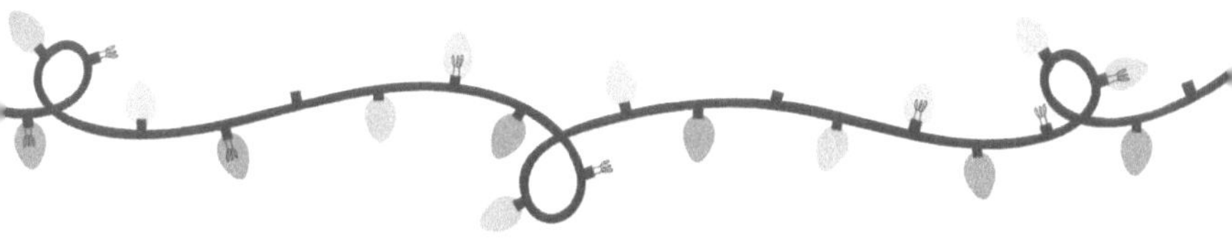

CHAPTER TWO

Chelsea Moore never got hangovers.

Except, apparently, when she drank a bar dry in an attempt to forget what a tailspin her life had taken. She didn't open her eyes as she pressed her fingertips against her throbbing temples. Aubs came up with the brilliant idea of going out to celebrate, even though the divorce wouldn't be official until the six-month mark—only four more to go. Her sister had hated her ex-husband from the start, a trend that continued the longer they were married. When Noah's negligence and negging reached a crescendo, the crack to her Liberty Bell had been his demand for them to move to Chicago for his job.

Fuck no.

She tentatively opened her eyes, wincing at the

bright sunlight streaming in through the windows. Chelsea lay in a bed that wasn't hers, wrapped up in a warm gray down comforter with Jersey knit sheets beneath her. Her stomach churned a bit, but her head was the victim here. She'd lost count of the number of bottles of beer she'd tossed back last night. Chelsea glanced under the sheets. She'd ditched her socks and shoes but still wore her skirt and shirt, which meant she most likely hadn't tumbled into a one-night stand.

Even though her body protested, she pushed up from the bed, curiosity getting the better of her. She tugged at the hem of her skirt, which rode all the way up her thighs, and she headed for the door. A voice came from the other room... humming? She crept out into the narrow hallway, all bright and filled with sunshine like the room, its neat eggshell walls scattered with a few landscape pictures for decoration. Based on the glance out the window to the bustling city street a few floors below, she was still in Philly. Chelsea bypassed the bathroom until she peered around the corner into the open-space area featuring the living room and kitchen.

Kyle stood behind the stove, flipping bacon on the skillet, the delicious, salty smell wafting Chelsea's way. The woman hummed a tune to herself, dressed in a loose tank top and black shorts showcasing a stunning ass. Chelsea would be lying if she said she hadn't noticed before. She paused there, watching this private moment. A strand of Kyle's ear-length auburn hair slipped to the front of her face, and she blew at it, the motion adorable.

With her hazel eyes, straight nose, and graceful jawline, the woman was gorgeous as hell, a sparrow-like curiosity to her features. She shimmied in time to whatever tune she hummed, continuing to flip the bacon on the skillet. A grin rose to Chelsea's lips. The second she stepped into the room, Ky would be all flusters and embarrassment, but this glimpse of the woman was well worth waiting a minute or two.

Chelsea knocked against the wall before she strode in. "You have no idea how relieved I am to be here and not waking up in some frat-douche's bed."

Kyle almost jumped, a blush staining her cheeks as she whipped around to face her. "You're up already? How are you feeling?"

"Like I got hit in the head with the keg I must've tossed back last night," Chelsea murmured, stepping the rest of the way into the kitchen. Her stomach rumbled at the scent of the bacon filling the room.

"Hoping the hangover doesn't include nausea, because I made bacon, eggs, and toast," Kyle said, tilting her head toward the plates on the counter. "Coffee too. Basic breakfast is one of the few things I can reliably cook."

"Breakfast made? I should've married you, not my shitty ex-husband," Chelsea said, sweeping past her to clasp one of the full mugs of coffee to her chest. The heat from the mug imprinted on her palms, and she took the first glorious sip, hoping the warmth and caffeine would put a dent in this hangover.

"Aspirin and water are right there," Kyle said, gesturing to the counter with her spatula as she gathered the bacon from the frying pan and dispersed the contents between the two plates.

Chelsea snagged the cup of water and the two aspirin Kyle set out, tossing them back and chugging down the cool liquid. Gratitude flushed through her at the way this woman took care of her, offering more sweetness than she'd received through the duration of her marriage. That was Kyle Walker up and down though. How the woman wasn't snatched up by now mystified her, because she'd never forgotten who showed up at the hospital to bring takeout or just sit and read in the waiting room with her and Aubs through Mom's struggle with cancer.

"So, care to explain how I ended up here?"

Chelsea asked, leaning against the counter. "Everything got a bit hazy after I jumped onstage to do amateur burlesque."

Kyle ducked her head, the blush lighting up her cheeks. "Yeah, no one managed to top your performance." The tension in the air between them thickened, and Chelsea cocked her head in curiosity. Before she could ask anything, Kyle continued. "Then we all proceeded to drink. A lot. And when Aubs was ready to ship you home, you told her if you got in a car you'd hurl. Then you explained that we were having a sleepover, since I lived right up the street."

Chelsea snorted. "Yeah, sounds about right. I'm sure my sister went apoplectic."

"I got a stern talking to, but that was about it," Kyle said, bringing the laden plates over to the small two-seater stationed in her kitchen. "And then I got you into the bed, and I took the couch."

Christ, this woman. She'd never met someone as genuinely caring as Ky, and she wouldn't again. Her brows drew together. "Wait, why'd you get the talking to?"

Kyle arched a brow, a blush spreading to her entire face. "Because we're both single women, and she seemed to think I'd try to jump you in the middle of the night or convert you to the gay."

"That ever-contagious gay." Chelsea rolled her eyes. "Aubrey's one to talk. Besides, I'd way rather wake up in bed next to you than half of the guys at the bar last night."

Until the words escaped her mouth, she didn't realize how suggestive they sounded. Right, that was going to go over great, flaunting herself in front of her sister's best friend. Not like the woman wasn't hot as fuck, especially all relaxed like this in her own environment. Kyle glanced away, letting out a slow breath. Chelsea's heart sped a little faster, probably from the coffee kicking in.

"Better dive into breakfast before it gets cold," Ky muttered, as if she wasn't trying to divert the conversation. "Cold eggs just taste like scrambled rubber."

Chels snagged a slice of bacon and began to chew, enjoying the salty flavors exploding on her tongue. When she added the buttered toast to the mix, she almost let out a groan. Breakfast might be simple to fix up, but this was cooked to perfection. The yolk of the sunny-side up eggs split, running across her plate, and she dipped the pieces of toast into it. The breakfast and coffee started to invigorate her, as if she wasn't roadkill in the wake of bad decisions.

Still, she refused to count her divorce as one. Marrying Noah, yes, that had been a grievous error on her part, but leaving him had been her best choice, even if Dad had been disgruntled about the whole thing the past few months.

"Did you have fun last night?" Chelsea asked, curious to have some of the blanks filled in. The outing had been necessary, a chance for her to let loose and declare her freedom to the world. "Sorry if me crashing here vag-blocked you or anything." She scratched her wild waves, more than aware she looked like a train wreck right now.

"Please. Me?" Ky responded, shaking her head. "Do I look like the type who's bringing home girls every night? Maybe like the type who owns a thousand dogs, but I don't play the field like that. I had a blast, mostly because you were so trashed it kept Aubs and Sky from trying to hook me up with any single lady they found at the bar."

"What would be so bad about that?" Chelsea asked, taking a sip of her black coffee. She'd known Kyle for years but never got a chance to talk with her one-on-one like this.

"If we could skip past the awkward introductions

where I say something horrifying, nothing. But I'm the least charming person in the tristate area, and I've scared more women away in the first five minutes than I can count."

"No fucking way," Chels said, shaking her head. She took a minute to wipe under her eyes, realizing her makeup probably streaked everywhere. "Sorry, I didn't even look in the mirror. I probably look horrible."

Kyle shook her head. "Nah, you're gorgeous." Her voice was so soft when she said those words in an earnest tone that made Chelsea melt.

"Wait, you're telling me women walk away from this?" she asked, circling her finger around as she pointed at Kyle. "Between the genuine grin of yours that would make hardened criminals weak in the knees and the way you put the people around you at ease, you're a freaking catch."

"I'm going to hope the earth swallows me up in the next five seconds so I don't die from embarrassment," Kyle said, taking a bite from her bacon all while avoiding Chelsea's eyes.

Kyle's tendency to dodge compliments and downplay herself never struck her before, but while talking one-on-one like this, she noticed immediately.

Kyle swallowed her bacon and glanced back up.

"Most women don't seem to agree. Whenever I meet someone new, rational conversation escapes my brain, and I end up telling them they've got great sternocleidomastoid muscles or ask if free will is real or just an illusion."

Chelsea pursed her lips. Disbelief coursed through her. How had no one found those questions charming? Everything about Kyle Walker was endearingly cute. Maybe her sister had the right idea after all. After Noah, the idea of hopping into bed with another guy made her gut roil.

"I'm back and forth on the free will thing," Chelsea commented, taking another bite of toast. "I think on an individual scale, we make our own choices, but I'm also a big believer in fate too—that some markers in history, in our lives, are predestined no matter how we try to combat them."

Kyle shook her head. "Well, you're the first person to give me an answer on that one. Most I got before was scrunched eyebrows and blank looks or a 'let me think on it' as they found somewhere else to be fast." She glanced at Chelsea, those hazel eyes beautiful and framed by thick lashes. "I'm in the same camp of thought though. I don't believe we're powerless, but I also have a hard time thinking everything is pure chaos, volatile and explosive."

"Not the conversation I expected upon waking up with a massive hangover, but I've got to say, you keep things interesting," Chelsea said, finishing the rest of the eggs on her plate and washing them down with a sip of coffee. This had been the best damn wake-up she could've hoped for after last night. Already, the effects of the coffee, aspirin, and water settled into place, clearing out a lot of the throbbing in her head.

Kyle's phone buzzed, and she glanced down. A low curse came from her that she fast tried to cover up by taking an extra big gulp of coffee.

Well, now she grew even more curious.

"Annoying text?" Chelsea asked. On her best day she couldn't help but pry—not because she was a gossip or anything, but her curiosity was as insatiable as her sex drive.

"My mother," Kyle grumbled. "I did something stupid, and now I'm kind of stuck in a weird situation."

Chels quirked her eyebrow up. "Oh?" she asked, which was all she volunteered. She wouldn't push, but she hoped Ky would elaborate. Getting to know Kyle Walker better was the most fun she'd had in months.

Kyle scrubbed at her face. "My folks aren't like...

the 'cast you out in the cold because you're queer' sort. But they're always nudging, asking if maybe I'd reconsider and try dating a guy. They're not antagonistic, but they're not supportive either."

"Right, sounds so like my dad. I'm sure Aubs has told you plenty," Chelsea stated, clutching the sides of her coffee mug.

Kyle nodded. "And I haven't brought anyone home—no relationships lasted long enough for me to feel comfortable taking them to my family get-togethers. So, when Mom started pushing about her setting me up with a guy for the Christmas get-together this year, I snapped and told her I'd be bringing my girlfriend."

"Who you don't have," Chelsea said, filling in the blanks. She let out a low whistle. "That is quite the conundrum, Ky."

"Tell me about it," she said, slumping forward to rest her forehead on her arms. "If my folks didn't already know my whopping two best friends, I might ask Aubs or Sky to pretend for me, but that option's shot. So, I've got to take this charming personality and try to find myself someone who isn't going to run in fear if I spring a family meeting on them a month into dating."

Chelsea's heart twisted. If her folks treated her

anything like Dad did Aubs, well, hell. His attitude had caused Aubrey's words to get sharper with every passing year, not to mention only added to her sister's long-time avoidance of real relationships—at least, until Selina. Watching Dad and Aubs go at it pretty much steered her rickety sailboat toward men early on, mostly because she didn't want to fight with him. Like that route went well. Her two-year marriage with Noah had ended up lit on fire and sent traveling down the river, Viking-funeral style.

She took another sip of her still-warm coffee and almost choked. The idea slammed into her. "What about me?" she asked.

Kyle glanced up, her brows scrunched in pure bewilderment. "Huh?"

"You said you can't use Aubs or Sky because your folks know them, but what about me? I'm free-wheeling and untethered in the dating scene, so you don't have to worry about any complications or frustrations with partners." As Chelsea made the suggestion, a hint of giddiness rose in her chest. There was a vindictive justice in being able to stick it to Kyle's dick parents, as if she might be able to stand up to Dad like Aubrey had been doing for years.

Kyle cocked her head to the side, which placed her slender neck on display. Those clavicles were pronounced, and a dusting of freckles across her nose and cheeks added to the plethora of unique features that made her so damn pretty. "Would you even feel comfortable doing something like that?" she asked, scratching the back of her neck.

Chelsea rolled her eyes. "What, hanging out and getting handsy with one of the best chicks I know? Sounds like a total hardship to me. I mean, I might need to get to know you a little better beyond 'Aubrey's best friend,' but hey, I can't think of better company in singledom."

Kyle speared her fingers through her hair, the sun from the windows bringing out the red and orange highlights, like gasps of flame. "Holy hell, Chels. You have no idea what a relief that would be. I shouldn't have even opened my mouth in the first place, but I'm just so sick of them trying to pretend away the gay, like if they hoped for long enough I'd cave on my sexuality to make life easier for them."

"Fuck that. We're going to be obnoxiously cute and in their faces," Chelsea responded, excitement bubbling in her chest. She'd been feeling a little aimless since the divorce, like the word "failure" was branded on her bones from here on out. But this could offer the perfect distraction, as well as a way to help a friend while she tried to heal.

Kyle glanced up at her, those hazel eyes softening and a bright, honest grin gracing her face. "Goddamn. Thank you, Chels." Her hushed tone caused Chelsea's heart to speed up a couple of notches. This was the right move to make if only to put that look on Kyle's face. The poor girl deserved the world and clearly hadn't received it.

Chelsea thrust out her hand. "So, it's agreed. For your big Christmas party, I'll be your fake girlfriend."

Kyle pressed her palm against hers, the skin soft yet her grip stronger than anticipated. "It's a deal."

A shiver coursed up Chelsea's arm at the contact. Curiouser and curiouser.

Chelsea offered a grin, all teeth. "This is going to be fun."

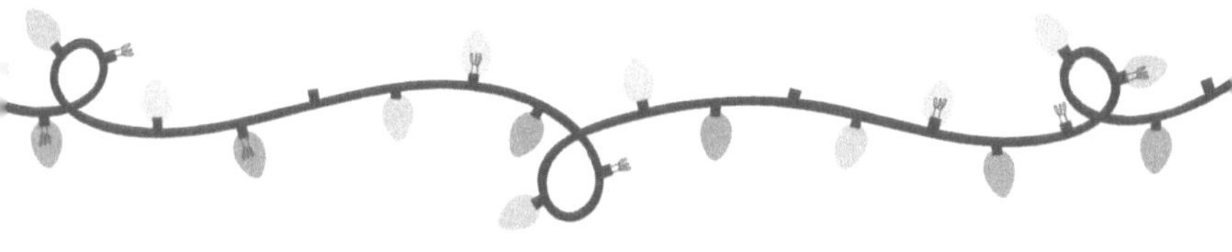

CHAPTER THREE

Friendship was the only reason in the world Kyle had gotten up at the ass crack of dawn on a Saturday to attend Aubrey's free outdoor kick-boxing session.

In November.

The woman was insane, but the demand for her classes reached an all-time high, and she had a ton of signups for this event. Even still, Aubs begged and pleaded for the crew to show up on the off chance everyone flaked once they figured out how damn cold the East Coast in November was. Kyle pulled into the parking lot of Rockford Park, right near the Rockford Tower, which was a tall stone pinnacle framed by spindly trees that lost their leaves.

Because it was winter, and no one but the insane did outdoor classes in the winter.

She glanced over at the small crowd gathered in front of the tower, a mix of familiar and unfamiliar faces. She caught sight of Aubrey, Mia, and then a few folks she didn't know, but Kyle found herself scanning the crowds a bit longer anyway.

Chelsea strutted up to the rest of the group, moving with the sanguine confidence she always commanded.

Okay, so maybe Kyle'd shown up for another reason today.

They'd exchanged numbers on the morning after her divorce party, and ever since then, they'd been texting each other nonstop. Chelsea was wittier than Kyle realized, with a bluntness that crept out when she got passionate about something, mostly the finer points of using combos in fighting games or why people who wore velour track suits should be vaulted out of existence. For the most part, Chels avoided talking about Noah. Kyle wouldn't push, either. She knew from experience how stubborn the Moore women could be.

She stepped out of her car, her nose wrinkling the moment the first bracing wind slapped her in the face. Why couldn't Aubrey host this at the gym? You know, with temperature-controlled rooms and a lack of windy interference? Kyle tugged on the end of her sleeves, wishing she'd brought her gloves, or a full-body jacket, or a space heater. Aubrey caught sight of her, waving wildly to gesture her over. No backing out now.

Kyle sauntered across the field, most of the grass in some stage of plant death, withered and wrinkled. The ground crunched beneath her sneakers, signaling that it was winter and she should be curled up in her bed with a warm coffee, a thick blanket, and a Netflix show to catch up on. Before she reached the rest of the crowd, Chelsea jogged over to her.

The woman looked like a cup of hot chocolate in a blizzard, even at seven in the morning. The idea of pretending they were dating had been far too tempting to resist, even if the whole thing ended up biting Kyle in the ass afterwards. Her heart might end up shattered, but she hadn't experienced this thrill in far too long. Chelsea's thick waves were pulled back in a braid, exposing her defined cheek-bones and jaw. Those full lips drew Kyle's attention every time, and her dark eyes glittered as their gazes met.

"I can't believe you showed," Chelsea said. "Aubs and I placed bets."

"Aubs should know better," Kyle said, jamming her hands a little deeper into her pockets. "If I make a promise, I keep it."

"Lofty words, but you're about the only person on this planet I've seen follow through, so I guess I better believe them." Chelsea crooked a finger in her direction, and Kyle's adrenaline kicked up like she was mid-run. When a hot-as-sin woman like that gestured at her, she couldn't help but follow.

Aubs hopped over to them, a wide grin on her face. "Ready to get your sweat on, Ky?" She had way too much energy for this time in the morning, like some hyper border collie.

Kyle wrinkled her nose. "Do I have a choice but to say yes?"

"That's the spirit," Aubs said, slapping her on the back, exuberance dialed to 110 percent. "Let's get rolling on warm-ups." With that, Aubrey skipped to the front of the pack and donned her drill sergeant voice. Kyle had attended a few of her classes before, and she always liked watching her bestie slip into her element. Sky and Selina both weren't in attendance, but given the early hour on a Saturday and the bar and restaurant jobs they worked, they were probably still asleep.

Kyle settled into place next to Chelsea in the back row.

"It's like we're the bad kids," Chelsea mock-whispered to her, those mischievous eyes glittering. "Think my sister's going to murder us by the end of this?"

The devilish look from Chelsea caused Ky's mind to whirl, even this early. The woman's presence detonated like a grenade of intensity, and the sheer strength of her focus sent Kyle floundering. It had been a long, long while since a woman this beautiful paid her any attention.

"I'm pretty sure if we're following your sister's drills, we'll be too exhausted to resist," Kyle responded, unable to hide her grin. Every interaction with Chelsea, even their texts, lightened something in her chest, some heavy sediment she hadn't realized settled there over time.

Within seconds, Aubrey barked out the first orders, and the drills began. Kyle tried to focus and move her body in time, but she'd never been coordinated. She lagged a step or two behind and tripped over herself a couple of times when her gaze drifted to the woman by her side. Chelsea pivoted and twisted with each instruction, smooth and fluid. Apparently, athletic coordination ran in the family. Chelsea's braid whipped around behind her, and the way her body turned was mesmerizing. Whether she stripped down in a bar or executed perfect jabs, crosses, and uppercuts, the woman looked gorgeous doing it.

Kyle needed to get this crush under control, pronto.

Not only was Chelsea Aubrey's little sister, but she was straight.

Kyle had been teased enough by straight friends in high school after she came out, female friends who all of a sudden got weird with her, making snide comments to stop drooling over them, or to keep her hands to herself. Each comment caused another slice to her skin until she'd gotten so marked up it was hard to find any smooth surfaces.

She zoned into the repetitions during the class until her muscles burned and droplets of sweat coursed down her forehead, sliding down her neck and back. The cold still numbed her nose, but the bitter breeze wasn't bothering her as much anymore. She could appreciate workouts like this in the same way she lost herself in the fluid movements of massage. The faint sunlight trickled through the cragged tree limbs, and even the skitter of a few skeletal leaves blowing across the asphalt behind them didn't distract her like they did at the start.

She couldn't help but sneak glances over to Chelsea during the entire class. They needed to get a crash course on each other in a month, the count-down starting from now until the Walker Family Christmas Bash. Even though the anxiety of trying to pick up someone on Tinder or at the bars in the time-frame had dissipated, a new tension threaded through. Chelsea had always been in a relationship ever since she'd known her—most of the time with Noah.

The more time Kyle spent with this woman, the more her mind took flight to Neverland, sailing away on fantasies that could never happen. And yet, with the way the barren-park loneliness crept in as of late, she couldn't find the strength to shut it down either.

"And walk in place, back and forth, back and forth," Aubrey called out, her voice as crisp as the surrounding air. "Shouldn't be hard to cool down in these temps."

Kyle shook her head, biting the inside of her cheek.

Chelsea nudged her in the side. "Ignore my

sister's poor attempt at humor. All this sweat is going to turn to ice fast."

"So, you're saying we should make a run for the car before she gets some other brilliant idea in her head?" Kyle grabbed the bottle of water she'd brought and downed a third in one go. The liquid rushed through her, but Chels was right—she'd freeze in minutes.

Aubrey shouted out the end of class, all bright, peppy encouragement, and everyone began to wipe their faces with towels, sleeves, or whatever was accessible. A few in the crowd shed their jackets, but Kyle didn't dare because she wanted to retain as much heat as possible.

Mia jogged up to them. "Hey, I'm sorry I didn't catch you at the beginning of class."

Kyle shook her head. "I arrived just in time for things to kick off. Trying to minimize my time in the great outdoors."

Mia checked her phone. "Sounds like Sky's got food prepared back home, so I better get going. Let's make some plans soon, yeah?"

Kyle barely nodded before she hugged Mia, who bolted off moments later. She cast a glance to Chelsea, whose lips were pursed, a thoughtful expression on her face. Kyle wanted nothing more than to grab breakfast with a friend, but Aubs would probably be vacating Rockford Park to head home to Selina after this, wanting to spend time with her lady love. Kyle didn't blame her, but damn, the reality sucked.

"My sister's got to wrap with these folks and then she's en route to wake up Selina," Chelsea said, her gaze knowing.

Kyle's chest sank before she could help it. She was happy for them, damned happy, but as always, she got picked last, whether for sports teams or coupling up in their group.

Chelsea hadn't looked away from her, the corners of her lips curling up. "I'm starving, though, and need breakfast. Want to grab brunch with me?"

Ky's heart sped, and she nodded before she could help herself. "Fuck yes."

Chelsea's grin widened. "Great. I'll meet you at Roadside Café. It's about five minutes from here." With that, she strode in Aubrey's direction. "Oi, Brea-gol," she called, her voice carrying with the breeze. "I'm out. See you later."

Kyle bit back her smirk. She'd heard Chelsea's *Lord of the Rings* riff on her sister's name a few times before, but Aubrey promised swift and sudden death if any of them attempted to use it on her.

Aubrey waved, midconversation with one of her clients. Her gaze landed on Kyle, and a second later, she excused herself and jogged over. Kyle's heart pounded. She should tell Aubrey about the deal she and Chelsea made, but she didn't want things getting uncomfortable. Aubs got growly bulldog protective over her little sister, and neither Kyle nor Chelsea needed the heat right now.

"Hey, Ky," Aubs said, clapping a hand on her shoulder and squeezing. "I've got to go after this, but I wanted to say thanks for showing up. It meant a lot to me."

Kyle forced a grin. "No problem." Even still, a twist in her chest accompanied all of these changes. Just a year ago, she and Aubrey would be grabbing a breakfast sandwich at Lucky's together and swapping stories, but that happened less and less frequently as of late. "I'll try to swing by Renegades soon."

Aubrey broke into a bright grin the way she did any time someone mentioned her girlfriend's bar. "That'd be perfect." She bit her lip, glancing off to the side before her gaze landed on Kyle. Pity. Great. "Sorry if I haven't been around as much. I'm not used to this whole balancing a relationship thing."

Ky shook her head, keeping a smile frozen in

place. "We're all square, Aubs. Commitment is a good look on you. I've got to grab breakfast now or I'll chew my arm off though. See you later."

She shoved her hands into her pockets and headed for the car. One thing right now took off the sting—Chelsea was waiting for her at Roadside Café, and honestly, that caused her mind to whirl in a way she hadn't allowed in a long while.

Kyle hopped into her car and blasted the heat, her fingertips tingling as they melted. By the time she'd pulled out of her parking spot, she began to feel the rest of her body again, even if her toes remained numb. Hopefully by the time she reached Roadside Café she could get into the right headspace. Going out for brunch with Chelsea Moore had her tangled up, and she tried her best to ignore the guilt tugging at her heels.

Friends. They were meeting for a nice, friendly date. Filled with friendship, not the other F-word that kept creeping into the back of her mind. Even if Chels swung her way, a gorgeous woman like her would never go for Kyle. Totally out of her class.

Kyle put her foot to the pedal, speeding up as she swerved onto the highway, en route to the café. Each minute closer she got, she didn't know whether nerves or anticipation would consume her first.

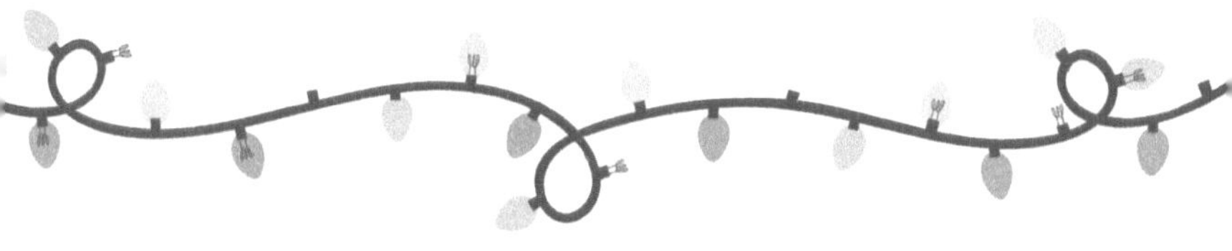

CHAPTER FOUR

Chelsea sat in the two-seater at Roadside Café, trying to drown out the odd sensation that swept over her by staring at the colorful purple walls with the lime trim. She still hadn't adjusted to going to places like this by her lonesome. When she'd been with Noah, she'd pulled away from so many of her friends that she'd gotten used to going everywhere with him, like one of those koala pencil toppers with the ultra-tight grip. She hadn't realized how much he controlled with his subtle comments, how one by one, he'd encouraged her to distance from people she'd been friends with forever.

Now, her pride was the one thing keeping her from reaching back out.

She checked her phone for the fifth time since

she sat down. What if Ky bailed on her? She'd asked the woman here on a spur of the moment decision after seeing the flash of pain in Kyle's eyes when Mia said she was heading out. Now on the frosted-glass outside of being in a couple, she'd come to realize how lonely this could be—part of the reason why she'd stayed with Noah as long as she did.

These jitters over meeting a friend for brunch were brand-new too. Normally, she'd barely blink over grabbing breakfast, lunch, or dinner with someone—apart from going on a date. Around her, a few patrons took up some of the other seats, all lovey-dovey couples, which should've made her sick, or sad. Instead, the sight made her feel a little wistful. Not for what she'd had, because her marriage had been destined for a dumpster fire, but for what she might've experienced if she'd waited for the right person.

The door creaked open, and Ky stepped inside. The woman looked a little lost as she scanned the tables, her short auburn hair rumpled from the wind and her cheeks pink from the chill outside. Chelsea's adrenaline kicked up a notch, something she willfully ignored as she lifted her hand to wave. Ky's gaze snagged on hers, and those hazel eyes crinkled with one beautiful grin.

Chelsea had grown used to a world of guarded expressions, smooth comments, and extra doses of sarcasm, but there was something different about Kyle Walker. The woman might hide behind awkwardness and fumbling, but when she smiled at her—holy hell, the sight knocked the breath from her chest so hard her ribs rattled. Not a sensation she was used to in the slightest, and one she should probably examine a bit more if she were honest with herself, which she didn't often like to be.

"If we do this whole chatting over breakfast a third time, it's going to become tradition," Chelsea said as Ky approached. She nudged out the chair opposite to her.

"Breakfast is a worthy meal for traditions," Kyle said as she took the seat and began scanning the menu. "Thanks for inviting me out in the first place. This was a great interruption to my prior plans of heading home to sulk."

"Not going to lie, I forgot what a headache it is to plan things like brunch when you're single. You can't just roll out of bed and drag your partner along with," Chels said. Not like Noah went with her much.

"Tell me about it," Kyle muttered. "I'd kill to have someone to grab brunch with on the regular.

Hanging out used to be a lot easier when Sky, Aubs, and I were all single, but it's gotten complicated lately."

Her hazel eyes darkened, and Chelsea's chest tugged hard.

"Well, as your fake girlfriend, I'm fine with making this a standing date," she said, offering a cheeky smile. She wanted to wipe the bit of sadness off of Kyle's features.

Kyle's lips quirked with a grin. "If I'd known fake girlfriends came with perks like breakfast dates, I would've gotten myself one of those years ago. Or, you know, fumbled my way through that too."

"You're a mystery, Kyle Walker," Chelsea said, tapping the cup of coffee in front of her.

A waitress swung by the table to grab their orders, and Kyle placed one for coffee and banana-stuffed french toast. Chelsea ordered a green pepper and cheddar omelet, and the waitress whisked off again with their menus.

Kyle crooked a brow at her. "I can't see how you're finding any mystery in all of this," she said, sweeping her arm down her torso. She'd ditched her jacket and zip-up hoodie, and her muscle tee left her bare, toned arms exposed. Chelsea couldn't help but take a second look, her gaze lingering on the definition in Kyle's biceps. She should also admit she'd scoped out Kyle's ass for at least half of the kickboxing class earlier today, but the self-confession could be addressed at another time.

"You, being single. That's the total mystery. You're a package made for commitment, so different from my sister when she hurled herself at any available pussy possible."

Kyle shook her head. "Beyond the plain looks factor, I'm as boring as they come. I've worked the same job for a million years, I will predictably order the sweetest thing on any brunch menu, and a Saturday filled with baking banana bread, cuddling, and Netflix sounds miserable to most and perfect to me."

Chelsea tried to stifle the flutter in her chest at the idea of a cozy weekend like that. She'd been unleashed into the wilds of singlehood again, but nights with Noah had been anything but comfortable. Even when they were on the couch together, he was buried in his phone, and she was trying to escape into a game on her handheld—opposite ends of the couch and never touching. Most of their relationship was lonely, and she'd spent a lot of time going out to escape. "I haven't had homemade banana bread in years. I can cook, but baking's always eluded me."

"Really?" Kyle's features sparked to life. "Before I went into massage, I wanted to own a cupcake store for a hot stint. At least I did until I found out the early hours that came along with the job and how the professional aspect would leech a lot of the joy from the hobby for me. No regrets here though, because I love my line of work."

Chelsea started ticking off her fingers. "Massage therapist, can bake cupcakes, and a total hottie? Yeah, it's a definite mystery as to why you're still single."

A flush rose to Kyle's cheeks again, one Chelsea fast found adorable. To be honest, half of the time she said provocative things just to witness Kyle blush all over again. It was addictive.

"Do you mind if I ask a question?" Kyle asked, curiosity in her gaze.

"I'll answer anything as long as it doesn't have to do with Noah or the divorce," Chelsea shot back. She'd been eluding everyone's attempts at discussing the topic, Aubs's especially, but she couldn't bring herself to take a spade and dig past the surface right now. Not because she missed him—God, how she didn't miss him—but this wasn't just a misstep in her life plan. This was a full tumble down the steps.

Kyle's brows drew together. Clearly, she'd been

thwarted. The woman pursed her lips as she met her gaze again. "What are you looking for now that you're out there again?"

She'd managed to find a question that dodged around both her ex and the divorce. Clever. Kyle chose a good one too, and while lies bubbled to her lips, she found she didn't want to use them.

"If and when I date again," Chelsea started, "I'll do a lot of things differently. Noah was hot and we were fire in the sheets at first, so I didn't ask too many questions and just dove in like a kid at the ball pit."

The waitress swung over with their orders, placing the coffee and stuffed french toast in front of Kyle and the omelet in front of her. Chelsea stole those moments to douse her omelet in ketchup and mull over what she would say next.

Kyle lifted her cup of coffee to her mouth, taking a sip. Chelsea's gaze lingered at the liquid glossing the perfect Cupid's bow of those pink lips. Kyle didn't say anything, but her gaze still focused on Chelsea as she waited for her answer.

"I'd take the time to get to know my partner next time around," Chelsea said, averting her gaze as she sliced into her omelet. "Make sure we have the kind of compatibility that's more of a steady hearth than a firework. With Noah all the great sex faded quick, and being married to someone who barely understands you is lonelier than being by yourself."

Chelsea lapsed into silence, not voicing the two secrets she kept to herself.

Sex got awkward between her and Noah once she realized she possessed a dominant streak that wasn't being sated. Noah was your average meat-head, not willing to dip his toes into the world of BDSM, and definitely not willing to submit. She'd kill to find a play partner and explore.

And the second secret—well, she hadn't even accepted that one with herself quite yet.

"Maybe if I took a chance on some fireworks, I'd get laid a little more," Kyle responded, offering a smile before she started into her overly sugary concoction. "My last one-night stand was on our Rehoboth trip this past year while Selina and Aubrey were busy finding true love. Even with that one, I started to get attached. I'm like an octopus with all those little clingy feeler bits."

"You mean suckers?"

"Yeah." Ky nodded, a short laugh escaping her lips. "That about sums me up."

Chels chewed on her omelet, enjoying the bite of the cheddar and the juicy peppers. The sun streamed in through the windows, glowing down on her skin like it was summer, not the middle of November. "Don't talk those choices down. If I'd waited a little more, maybe I wouldn't be sitting here fresh out of a divorce." She lifted her fork, pointing the tines at Kyle. "What we do need to figure out, since we're both here, are the parameters of this whole fake-girlfriend gig."

"Parameters?" Kyle asked, her beautiful hazel eyes widening. "I mean, I figured we'd just show up to the family Christmas shindig and they'd back the hell off."

Chelsea shook her head. "My sweet summer child. You do realize if I'm the first girl you're bringing home, I'm going to get grilled for sure. Especially if they don't want to believe you're gay. And we need the act to come across as believable if they're going to leave you alone, right?"

"Fuck, this is way more complicated than I thought it'd be." Kyle speared another couple of syrupy bites of her stuffed french toast and chewed.

"Like, what's our meet-cute? When did you fall for me? When did I first swoon over you?" Chelsea asked, amusement rising in her chest the more she poked.

Kyle spluttered on her coffee, and Chelsea's grin

widened. Teasing this woman was far, far too much fun.

"I don't watch nearly enough rom-coms to figure that out," Kyle muttered as she tried to fight the ruddy flush on her cheeks. "How about we don't change things too much. I'm not a good liar to begin with, and my family will see right through me."

"Well, I am recently divorced. We could tell them you took me home after my divorce party and screwed my brains out," Chelsea said, taking another sip of coffee. For a brief moment when she'd woken up in the strange bed that morning, she had wondered. And when she'd seen Kyle in the kitchen, her brain drifted a step further.

If Kyle had been red before, it paled compared to now. "Yeah, that works. Though we can omit the 'screwing my brains out' part around my family, unless we want shit to get even more uncomfortable."

"Which brings us to PDA," Chelsea said, steamrolling ahead. Her sadistic side took too much delight in eliciting those delicious blushes from Kyle. She didn't know if the woman was in the lifestyle or not, but if Chelsea had to place bets, Kyle would be an amazing submissive. "What sort of public displays are you used to with your partners? Holding hands? Casual touches? Kisses?"

Even as she said the word, she couldn't help how her gaze drifted to Kyle's lips. The woman possessed a gorgeous mouth and probably tasted just as syrupy sweet as her breakfast.

Kyle glanced up at her, giving her a pointed, though amused, look. "If you're trying to make me immolate on the spot, you're doing a good job. I get embarrassed talking about this stuff. But honestly, whatever's comfortable for you, Chels. You're the straight one, so nothing that would make you feel squicky."

Chelsea lifted a brow. "Oh honey, please. Very little squicks me out—apart from guys who remind me of my ex-husband."

Kyle shook her head in disbelief. "You're something else, Chelsea Moore."

Something else was right on the money, because even before she'd left Noah, she'd found herself growing more and more curious.

And the more time she spent around Kyle with all her adorable blushes, sheepishness, and the honest smile that stole her breath away, the more curious she became.

CHAPTER FIVE

TRUE TO HER WORD, AUBS PLANNED A HANG night at Renegades the following Saturday while Selina worked. Relief flooded through Kyle's veins the moment she got the text, like they'd vaulted back into the old days when Aubs always hit up Renegades to hunt for some loose and lonely women. Mia was swinging out, and Sky would head over to join them all after her shift at work.

Kyle pulled into place right in front of the bar in downtown Wilmington. Finally, they'd get a chance to hang out. Not like she'd been feeling quite as lonely as of late. She'd been texting Chelsea throughout the week, finding out all the stupid things girlfriends should know about each other, even down to her bra size and favorite Pokémon. They'd gone to brunch at Roadside Café this morning, which at three times a charm officially made their weekend breakfasts a tradition. Between their time together and the way Chelsea practiced her PDA, brushing her fingers across Kyle's and touching her at any opportunity, she was feeling dizzy from all that contact.

Chelsea had been a distraction from everything, honestly. From the feelings of abandonment she'd been wrestling with, the complications between her and her family, and the ever-oppressive singledom that reminded her she'd end up living by her lonesome at forty with four corgis nipping at her heels.

She strode up to the lit Renegades sign, a classy bar with the prerequisite rainbow flag in the window. The deep bass of lively music pulsed from inside, the joint hopping even though the sun had barely just set. The one thing that had her nervous was if Aubs dropped into Ms. Fix-It mode and wanted to spend all her prime women-hunting energy into finding Kyle one.

Kyle speared her fingers through her auburn strands, a bit of a tousled mess from work anyway. She came straight from a day of massages, so she still wore her all-black attire comprised of leggings and a tunic with some comfortable sneakers.

The moment she stepped inside, the scent of cinnamon and clove greeted her from the upside-down herbal arrangements Selina positioned around the place, her own witchy blend of potpourri. The bar was fairly full already, and as Kyle scanned the line-up, she caught sight of Aubrey at one of the stools talking to someone who definitely wasn't Mia.

Kyle pursed her lips as she strode closer. Whoever Aubrey chatted with had long, smooth legs she wouldn't mind losing herself between and a gorgeous ass. Chances were, she'd bolt once Kyle stepped up to join them.

Aubrey caught sight of her and waved. As she did, the woman by her side turned around too.

Chelsea, of course. The woman's gaze locked on hers, and Chelsea's grin widened. Chels had changed since their earlier brunch, slipping into a crimson dress that hugged her ass and black leggings and knee-high boots straight out of Kyle's fantasies. Her rich chestnut hair lay in tumbles across her shoulders, and the dim lighting of Renegades high-lighted her sepia skin.

"Hey, Ky," Chelsea said, crooking her fingers as she beckoned her over. Fuck, the simple gesture sent her body into overdrive. The woman seemed to take sadistic delight in teasing her, but the more Chelsea did it, the more Kyle could swerve past the awkwardness and find her words. "You didn't say you were coming here tonight. Aubs told me I needed to get my ass out of the apartment because I clearly have no friends or plans."

Ky's lips quirked with her grin. Sounded exactly like Aubs. Except with both of the sisters in the same bar, she wasn't just playing with a flame—she'd thrust her whole hand into the fire. As long as Chelsea behaved and Kyle didn't drool over her too much, they might be able to avoid Aubrey's attention. Easy enough—Aubs wasn't as perceptive as her eagle-eyed girlfriend.

She strode up to the bar and offered Aubs a huge hug. "Thanks for setting this up," Kyle murmured.

Aubs flashed a huge grin. "See, I'm not a total asshole."

When Kyle turned around to face Chelsea, the woman held her arms open for a hug, and Kyle couldn't help but tumble forward. The deep inhale of the woman's almond-and-leather musk made her squeeze her thighs together, a thrill coursing through her body. She lingered a moment in the embrace, feeling the solidness of Chelsea's arms and how the woman gripped possessively.

Fuck, if only.

She pulled back with a weak smile and sidled up to the bar where Selina was hard at work swerving from one task to the next. The woman caught sight of her and winked. The curvy bar owner moved with perfect grace as she grabbed a glass.

"G&T, doll?" Selina asked, already pouring the gin and then spraying the tonic in.

Ky offered a thumbs up. Most of her friends knew her deal backwards and forwards at this point. Never the person to shake things up, she stuck to her tried and trues. She was the stable one, and most times, she didn't mind.

Just sometimes, she wished she could let loose. As if she could be wild or irresponsible and folks would love her in the aftermath, mistakes and all.

Kyle hopped on the extra stool beside them, and a minute later, a gin and tonic slid her way. Aubrey blew a kiss to her girlfriend, who sashayed away, offering a seductive glance back.

Kyle took a quick sip, letting the alcohol soothe her nerves. She glanced at Chelsea. "Why did your sister think bringing you to a gay bar was a good idea?"

Chelsea snorted. "Aubrey claims this was for my sake, but I think she wanted company while she sat at the bar pining for her lover all night."

Aubrey flipped her the middle finger. "Next time I'll take you to a straight bar where you can mash faces with all the guys you want, little sis. As long as I'm not looking."

"What about the Red Door?" Chelsea grinned, all teeth. "Would you take me there?"

Aubrey rolled her eyes. "You can do whatever you want, but I'm not bringing my baby sister to a kink club."

Kyle took another quick sip from her gin and tonic, not missing how Chelsea's gaze snuck toward hers. Her pulse quickened at the idea of the kink club, a place she'd always wanted to check out but never had the stones to. "The one in Philly, right?" she asked, even though she already knew. "I'd check it out."

Aubrey blinked at that one, whipping her head as she turned to face her. "You, Kyle? Queen of Vanilla Cupcakes?"

Kyle bit back her smirk. "Just because I don't sleep around a ton doesn't mean I'm pure vanilla." She'd never been in a Domme and sub relationship before, but from the glimpses she'd read about, the idea of getting bossed around sounded like a dream. The perfect way to pull herself out of her head and her own anxieties.

Aubrey shook her head. "Yeah, I'm not going with you either, Ky. You might as well be a sister. It'd be weird seeing you bound up and shit."

"No one asked you to, babe," she responded, taking another sip from her gin and tonic. When she glanced up, Chelsea's gaze was boring into her with an intensity to make her breath snag in her throat. If she didn't know better, she'd say there was a raw hunger in her expression, one that caused Ky to squeeze her thighs tighter. Hell, a look like that and she'd be willing to do anything the woman asked.

Guilt flushed through her again, and she looked away before Aubrey noticed she was flat-out ogling her sister. Guaranteed that wouldn't go over well.

"What I can do is help you scope out some prime real estate here," Aubrey said.

Kyle elicited a groan. "I'm not ready for my night to get ruined yet. Remember how the last five times went when you tried to wingman for me? Two of the girls asked for your number instead, and the other three managed a few minutes around me before they offered a polite smile and made an excuse about having to go to the bathroom, only to sneak out to a different part of the bar."

Mia strolled in through the bar doors, dragging the attention her way. Kyle sucked in a silent breath of relief. Aubrey just wanted to help in the one way she knew how. Except trolling the bar never worked for any of them in terms of finding "the one," especially not Aubrey. And Kyle hated how insecure each rejection made her feel, all the self-loathing she pinned back bursting free again and again.

Aubs hopped up from her seat and strode to meet Mia midway while Kyle and Chelsea held down the fort.

Chelsea leaned in close enough that her lips almost brushed Kyle's ear. She forced back a shiver.

"If you don't want to chase after women at the bar all night, I can thwart my sister," Chelsea murmured.

"Please and thank you," Kyle muttered. "I know she's worried about me, but a girl can only take so much of a beating."

Chelsea quirked a brow. "Depends on what sort."

Desire flooded through her at that throaty comment from Chelsea. After the way the conversation skated over BDSM earlier, she got the gist loud and clear.

"I was serious earlier," Kyle responded. "If you wanted someone to join you at the Red Door, I'd go. I've been trying to work up the nerve for years, but

I'm like a turtle half the time, and new experiences make me duck back into my shell again. If I wasn't going by my lonesome, I could manage. I think."

"Don't tempt me, sugar," Chelsea purred. "I may take you up on the offer."

Kyle's nipples hardened beneath her shirt at the sensuality in the tone. Everything this woman did turned her on, yet Chelsea was oblivious to all of it. She'd probably get grossed out if she knew how much her flirty comments affected Kyle.

Mia and Aubs made their way over, and Kyle straightened in her seat, trying to act as if she wasn't turned on as hell right now. Hiding this from Aubrey was almost as tough as one of her kick-boxing classes, and yet this connection with Chelsea was keeping her afloat right now when little else did. With the holidays coming, the cozy, couple things she missed out on bombarded her on a daily basis, like getting ready for shared Thanksgivings, planning Christmas gifts for her partner, or even just snuggling indoors with a movie on a chilly night.

Normally she shook off those feelings, but with the rest of her best friends coupled up while she remained out in the cold, dwelling had become a perpetual state of being.

All of her tough luck in dating served as reminders of the lessons her mother served early on.

You're going to have to rely on something else besides your looks, sweetheart.

Just because her mom had been a model in her youth didn't mean that was a normal thing, genetics or no. Yet the woman didn't seem to understand that no amount of criticism or dieting was going to make Kyle's hips shrink or give her more symmetrical features.

"All right, now that Mia's here she can help search for a suitable chick for you to hit on," Aubs said, settling back in the seat.

"Or you could not bore your beloved sister to tears by spending the night as Kyle's unwanted wingman," Chelsea responded, just as loud as her sister. The two women were a force of nature in different ways. Aubrey burned hot like an inferno while Chelsea's intensity had a more hypnotic quality, like staring into the depths of a chasm.

Aubrey's brows drew together. "What else do people do at bars?"

"Beyond mooning over their girlfriends or trying to pick up women?" Chelsea responded, her tone filled with sarcasm. "I heard there's a little thing called drinking and conversing with your friends."

Mia elbowed Aubs in the side. "It's what the rest of us have always done."

Kyle passed Chelsea a grateful grin as their gazes met. The woman nodded, an understanding in her eyes that twisted her in knots. Somehow, in the short time since Chelsea's divorce party, the woman had gotten to know her far better than anyone had in a long, long while.

The door creaked open again, and Sky strode in, dressed down in her work pants and a tank top with a mauve hoodie instead of the chef's jacket.

"Got out early," she called out as she approached them. Kyle's grin widened. The original gang was together at last.

"Since we're all here, we should figure out our Friendsgiving plans. It's coming up in a few weeks, and I want to make sure I don't double-book us or anything," Mia said, plunking herself on a stool and turning to face them.

A moment later, Sky approached with a pint in hand, and she leaned in to press a passionate kiss on Mia's lips, the sort to make Kyle writhe with envy. Straight best friend turned lover was the fucking jackpot, one she'd wished for time and time again. When she told one of her best friends how she felt back in high school, she'd gotten the exact opposite response.

Another rejection to drop into the bucket.

"Are you coming to Friendsgiving this year?" Kyle asked, glancing toward Chelsea.

Chelsea shrugged. "Depends on if anyone invites me or not. I know I'm swimming in friends and popularity right now, so who knows if I'll even be around." The sarcasm there held a bitter tinge that plucked at Kyle's heart. Aubs told her how Noah pretty much distanced Chels from most of her friends, and now the woman was still picking up the shattered fragments.

"What's with the two of you getting so personable?" Aubrey asked, glancing their way. Kyle froze, not daring to glance to Chelsea in case the other woman blurted out the whole fake-girlfriend thing.

"You mean what's with the two single ladies hanging out while everyone else is coupled up?" Chelsea shot back, cool as ever. The woman's control was something else.

Aubs shrugged and tipped back her drink. "Touché." She glanced over at Kyle again. "Just don't get any ideas about my baby sister. She's only interested in dick anyway."

Kyle took the moment to tip back her gin and

tonic, hoping the flush hadn't army crawled up to her cheeks yet. "Wouldn't dream of it," she forced out.

"Yeah, Chels, you should come to Friendsgiving," Sky said, as open and sweet as ever. "Ignore your sister being bristly."

Aubrey lifted a middle finger but didn't complain.

Selina happened to swing by their end of the bar, which took Aubrey's attention away from them. Kyle sucked in a sharp breath, not daring to glance over at Chelsea in case she burst into flames on the spot.

Chelsea leaned in and knocked their knees together. "Just so you know," she said, whispering in her ear. "My sister's not the thought police. Have any ideas you like."

Fucking hell. This woman was a sadistic minx of the highest order, and Kyle was going to turn to ash on the spot.

Those devilish lips curled into a smile, and Chelsea pulled away, but not without squeezing her shoulder. The way she touched and teased sent shivers racing down Kyle's spine. Even if the woman was being friendly, Kyle couldn't resist the fantasies flaring in her mind. As much as this whole fake-girlfriend arrangement was a terrible idea, the loneliness had been like an eraser to her penciled lines, rubbing away more and more of her with every passing day. She couldn't help but fall prey to this attention.

She just wanted to pretend for a little while longer.

Chelsea's knee brushed against hers one more time before she turned to mouth off at her sister. When Kyle looked up, Mia was focused on the bar, but Sky cast a curious look in her direction, glancing between her and Chelsea.

Kyle averted her gaze, not even sure how she'd respond if Sky tried to say something. Tonight would be awkward as hell, and she'd invited Chelsea to Friendsgiving, where things were guaranteed to get even more uncomfortable.

Chelsea was straight.

Chelsea was Aubrey's sister.

Chelsea was recently divorced.

And yet Kyle couldn't help but stumble headfirst into this connection that had somehow developed between them faster than most friendships.

She only hoped the crash and burn didn't destroy her afterwards.

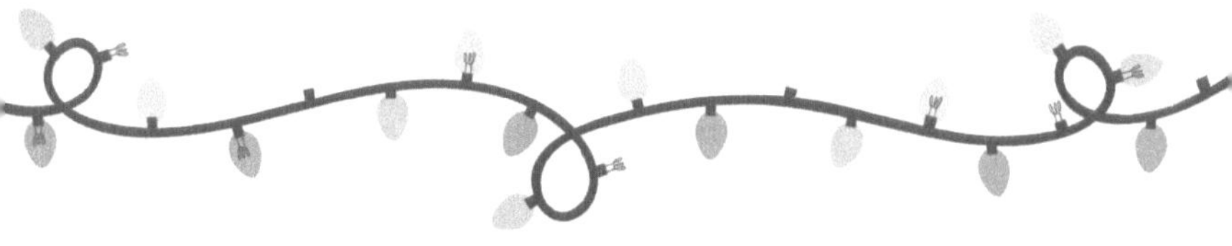

CHAPTER SIX

Somehow in the few weeks since her divorce party, Chelsea found herself in a routine. She put in her hours in the marketing department at work during the day, where she was currently assigned on an ad campaign for a new brand of headphones. Most of her free time, however, was spent bothering Kyle, whether via text, showing up randomly at her apartment, or going on their standing brunch date each Saturday.

If she were honest, this was the best she'd felt in years.

Being around Kyle was as natural as breathing, and she found herself dropping more and more barriers each time they hung out. The woman was more than cozy sweater comfortable—spending time with her felt like coming home after an exhausting day at work to a cooked meal. Though with the questionable way Kyle burned spaghetti, she'd be safer getting takeout.

"You didn't need to come grocery shopping with me," Kyle said again as they strode to the Whole Foods near her apartment. "I'm a big girl. I can do it myself."

"Yeah, but if I don't supervise, you might not pick up the supplies to make chocolate cherry cupcakes, and I'm pretty sure a promise was made," Chelsea said as she strolled beside her, arms swishing back and forth.

"I did promise to make them for you," Kyle said, a beautiful grin lifting her lips. "You know I'll follow through."

"Still, I'm here to keep you honest," Chelsea teased, enjoying the woman's responsiveness to every interaction. Ever since the night at Renegades when Kyle offered to join her at the Red Door, her mind had been whirring into overdrive.

Since she'd begun dating in high school, she'd always gone out with guys, and hell, she'd even married one. Truth be told, though, she'd be lying if curiosities hadn't crept in before. She'd even had crushes on female friends and coworkers that made her wonder.

And the idea of binding a woman in shibari ropes to eat out her pussy, of playing and teasing with gorgeous curves until her submissive was panting turned her on more and more as of late.

One woman starred in every single fantasy.

Kyle ran fingers through her hair before they entered. She was bundled in an army-green hoodie and leather jacket, yet her jeans couldn't hide the gorgeous ass that would look beyond beautiful pinked up at her hand or with a paddle. Chelsea bit her lip to restrain the impatient moan flowing through her.

Thoughts like those had ramifications. Big ones.

Yet she couldn't help but indulge in them anyway.

They stepped inside, the scents of bananas and fresh oranges greeting them as they strode through the produce section. Chelsea plucked at a couple of stray kumquats out of curiosity while they strolled along. Kyle popped some grapes and cherries into her basket before they headed down the row with the baking supplies. Chelsea walked a mere step behind Kyle, who fit perfectly in this aisle. The woman smelled like brown sugar and cinnamon, which captured all her sweetness so well.

Kyle scanned the shelves. "If you see the cocoa powder, grab it."

Chelsea reached past her for the tin of cocoa powder she'd spotted, making sure their arms brushed in the process. Was she pushing her flirtation into overdrive as of late? Yeah, to the point she should feel a little guilty. Yet she couldn't help herself. A brand-new thrill raced through her in response, and the need to sate her curiosity had begun to grow incessant.

"Here you go, sugar," she said, tossing the cocoa powder into Kyle's basket. She made sure to catch her eyes and wink in the process. Her reward was the delicious blush coating Kyle's cheeks in response. Kyle had started to build an immunity to some of her flirting, but whenever she caught her off guard, a raw, real reaction surfaced, and hell was it addictive.

"You're adamant about these damn cupcakes, aren't you?" Kyle responded, lifting a brow.

Chelsea's lips curled in amusement. "What can I say? Spending all this time around you is making me crave something sweet."

Kyle cast her a sidelong glance. "That was cheesy, even for you."

"Or it could have to do with the sheer amount of sticky sweetness you pour on your french toast. My God, are you trying to waterboard it in maple syrup?" Chelsea enjoyed their weekly brunch sessions far too much. Every time, she came out of them with some new tidbit about the woman, like the fact that Kyle refused to take Uber or a taxi because the drivers made her uneasy. Chelsea had seized upon that one for an entire day and a half. Kyle might brand herself as boring, but the way she owned the things she liked, how she stuck to routine, and how she followed her heart, made her one of the most interesting people Chelsea had ever met.

"I just like making sure each piece is coated," Kyle grumbled, plucking a bottle of vanilla extract from the shelves before she tilted her head to the next aisle down. Honestly, Chelsea hadn't been grocery shopping with someone else in so long, and she was enjoying herself. She and Noah mostly did groceries on their own, and if they took time to go together, the trip would end in a mid-aisle fight as they argued over what to eat. And not in the cute way.

They headed into the next aisle, and Kyle stopped so abruptly Chelsea slammed into her back.

A middle-aged woman strode over toward them

with a big grin on her face. "Kyle, it's been ages." She had a sort of hippy look to her with gray-streaked brown hair tugged into a loose bun, and she wore bright, summery florals in the middle of winter. A few crystal pendants dangled down her chest, and her tortoiseshell glasses only added to her bursts of color.

"Hey, Aunt Terry," Kyle said, her eyes widening as the woman came closer. She cast a panicked look to Chelsea.

Right, game time.

Before Aunt Terry could ask another question, Chelsea rested a hand on Kyle's shoulder and took a step closer in. The woman glanced between the two of them. "Who's your friend?" she asked.

"This?" Kyle asked, her voice a pitch higher, like the anxiety was a twister settling down in Kansas. "This is, ah, Chelsea."

Chelsea squeezed her shoulder. Time to take over. "Hey, I'm Kyle's new girlfriend." She took a step forward and offered her hand to shake. Chelsea delivered a blinder of a grin.

"Your mother said you might be bringing a date this year," Aunt Terry said, her eyes crinkling in mischief as she shook Chelsea's hand. "I'm glad you found someone brave enough to weather a Walker Family Christmas."

Chelsea had been bracing herself for a bucket of rudeness based on what Kyle warned her about most of the family. Aunt Terry must be one of the reasons Kyle still tried with the bunch of them.

"Ah, yeah," Kyle said. "She makes me really happy." The genuine look in Kyle's eyes sent Chelsea's heart pounding even faster. Warmth spread through her as she let go of Aunt Terry's hand and wrapped her arm around Kyle's shoulders. Kyle's raw affection couldn't be faked, and the sight struck her hard in the solar plexus.

"She's filling me in on what to expect before we go," Chelsea said, looking at Aunt Terry. "Quizzing me and all."

"Sounds like our Kyle," Aunt Terry said warmly, the lines of her face crinkling with amusement. "She always likes to be prepared."

"Guys, I'm right here," Kyle muttered, a ruddy flush lighting her cheeks again. The woman sank into her arms, and Chelsea found herself leaning in a little closer. Unable to help herself, she pressed a light kiss to the side of Kyle's head, her lips brushing against those glossy strands. Everything with Kyle Walker felt more comfortable than she could've imagined, whether it was holding hands or casual touches. The woman probably cuddled like a dream too. What she hadn't expected were the sparks that followed, licking up and down her spine as she pulled away.

"What she needs to prepare are those chocolate cherry cupcakes she promised me," Chelsea said, the words rolling off her tongue a little fast to hide how much the simple touch affected her. Curiosity burned inside to the point she'd been able to think of little else all week beyond those fantasies that grew more and more creative with every pass.

Kyle shot her a glance, her blush lighting her whole face this time. "You know, the more you mention them, the longer it's going to take for me to get around to making them."

Chelsea pursed her lips, and Aunt Terry let out a belly laugh, saying, "I won't keep you from your cupcakes any longer, Chelsea. It's wonderful to meet you though. Anyone who makes our Kyle so tongue-tied and happy is good in my book."

Now was Chelsea's turn to flush. She normally had no compunction in dodging around the truth, but this façade made her feel a little guilty. Kyle deserved the real deal more than anyone she knew.

"Great meeting you too," Chelsea said, her voice

softening. When she made this arrangement with Ky, she wanted to do a friend a favor. Kyle had seemed miserable and anxious about the prospect of facing her family alone at the Christmas gathering, and she could use a little bit of back up.

But the more she got to know Kyle, the more Chelsea realized she might be doing her a disservice in the long run. This woman was destined for happiness, even if she didn't see it yet. The way she checked in on her every morning with a text, how she made sure Chelsea was bundled up and comfortable when they hung out at Ky's place, and even the way Kyle had started trying to learn more about the video games Chelsea unwound to, asking questions with a ridiculous attentiveness—the woman was one of a kind.

"See you at Christmas, Aunt Terry," Kyle called out as her aunt began to wheel her cart in the opposite direction. The moment Aunt Terry disappeared into the next aisle, Kyle sank against the shelves. "Well, that was a close call." She glanced at Chelsea, a helpless noise escaping her throat. "Thanks for diving in there. I almost screwed up the whole plan. Clearly, I'm not a great liar."

"Hey, what are fake girlfriends for?" Chelsea asked, hoping Kyle didn't notice the strain in her voice or how her looks lingered as of late. The last thing Ky needed was a hot mess fresh out of a divorce who was questioning her sexuality. "Your aunt seems cool though."

"Apparently fake girlfriends are great for bailing me out of awkward family situations," Kyle said, even though her grin didn't meet her eyes. "Aunt Terry's one of the reasons I put up with the rest of the family at all. Her and my little brother Jake. Neither of them have been on the judgment brigade, and I know Jake would be heartbroken if I just ditched everyone."

"How old is Jake?" Chelsea asked as she reached for the laden basket Ky clutched onto, extricating it from her hands. She could take a turn carrying the weight.

Kyle pushed up from her slouch against the racks, and together they continued on down the aisle as she plucked more groceries to pop into the basket. "He's only twenty. Eight years younger than me and at school at Drexel. The kid's wicked smart."

"Does most of your family live in the city?" Chelsea asked, curiosity getting the better of her. They'd discussed so much, yet she hadn't even known Ky had a little brother. Aubrey didn't mention Ky's family much, but she'd come to realize Ky didn't either.

"We're sprinkled all throughout Philly and the suburbs," Kyle said, skimming her fingers through her hair again and again over the spot Chelsea had kissed earlier. The motion did something funny to her chest.

Aubs would kill them if she knew about any of this, but honestly, Aubs wasn't the person she worried about. Dad had always been in her corner, there with a smile and a hug, even through her fuckups and this divorce.

But what if the curiosity she brimmed with turned into something real?

Well, over the years she'd seen the Antarctic-sized glaciers that had grown between Dad and Aubs ever since she came out.

"What else is on the list?" Chelsea asked, needing the distraction. The more her thoughts lingered in that direction, the more her stomach did aerobatic dips. "With the amount you've already picked out, you'll need help carrying groceries to your apartment. This shit is heavy." She lifted the basket.

Kyle grabbed the basket back with a smirk. "I've got massage therapist muscles, so I can handle some weight. But if you're so desperate for those cupcakes, I won't say no to company on the walk back."

Chelsea's gaze lingered on the defined muscles of Kyle's neck, the firm shoulders, and muscular thighs. The woman made her pulse speed up every time.

They headed down the aisle with the different bars of chocolate, and Chelsea's eyes drifted to chocolate-chili. Her absolute favorite.

Kyle followed her gaze, and a moment later she reached up and snagged the bar. "In case we want something to snack on while we're walking back."

Goddamn, she might swoon.

Chelsea couldn't help the fluttering that coursed through her, something completely foreign after the years she'd slogged away with Noah.

They headed to the line, and her mind whirred into overdrive. Her mouth spoke for her before she could rein herself in. "What are you doing next Saturday night?" she asked.

Kyle looked at her, those hazel eyes filled with a wonder and curiosity Chelsea wished she could capture. "Nothing on the agenda yet. Why?"

Chelsea pursed her lips, about to bite back her stupidity, but her mouth kept running anyway. "Want to check out the Red Door with me? They're supposed to have a happy hour going on with a couple of public exhibitions."

Kyle's tongue trailed along her lip. "Yeah, sounds good. Let me know what time."

Chelsea's throat dried. Those fantasies she'd been replaying over and over again rushed to the forefront of her mind. Bringing Kyle to a place like that wouldn't help tamp them in the slightest, but she'd already stumbled forward before she could help herself.

Maybe she'd find a different submissive to play with, and Kyle might find a Domme interested in her. That thought made her gut churn. The only person Chelsea was fooling was herself.

The one woman she wanted to play with happened to be standing right next to her.

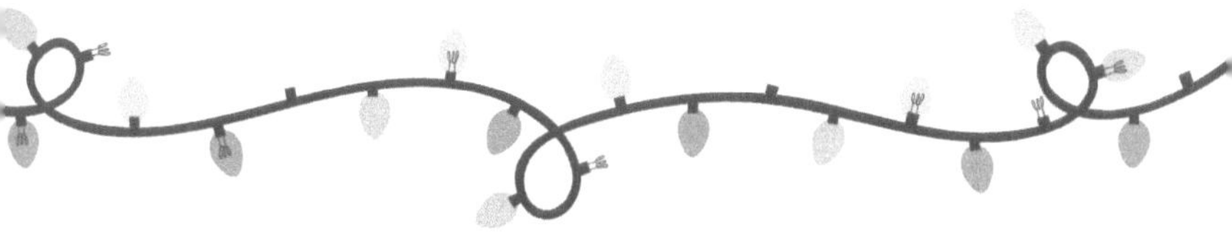

CHAPTER SEVEN

Kyle had been excited and terrified for this night all week from the moment Chelsea asked her to go. She'd wanted to experiment, but the idea of heading into something intense and brand-new only to get rejected there too prickled under her skin. Each and every turn-down just reinforced the lesson learned early on that she'd have to work extra hard to find anyone willing to settle for someone as plain as her.

She wasn't sure what the hell to wear to a BDSM club, but she didn't have leather pants to squeeze into, nor would she feel comfortable drawing attention to herself like that. Kyle settled for a hip-hugging pair of jeans, tank top, and open gray button-down, as well as her trusty leather jacket. She'd thrown on a bit of mascara, but that summed up what she could accomplish in the makeup department.

A knock pounded at her door. The sound sent a thrill coursing through her.

Even though they'd been meeting up for brunch on the regular and hanging out any spare second they could, tonight felt different.

Tonight felt like a date.

Kyle strode to her front door, trying to ignore the phantom carousel of touches and caresses Chelsea doled upon her every time they came close. She had to fight really hard to suppress the memory of the playful kiss Chelsea had dropped to the side of her head when they'd run into Aunt Terry. She'd nearly died on the spot. Her throat dried as her hand rested on the knob.

Going to the Red Door with Chelsea was dangerous.

She'd always liked Chelsea from the moment she met her, but Aubrey's little sister had been off-limits for a multitude of reasons. Yet ever since the divorce party, Kyle had begun to feel very different and far less innocent sensations any time she glanced in the woman's direction. And with the dozens of times Chelsea showed up at her door simply to crash on the couch and hang with her all night and how they'd gone from casual acquaintances to best friends in mere weeks—fuck, it made her head spin.

Kyle tugged open the door to Chelsea, who waited on the stoop.

She swallowed hard. The woman had pulled her hair into a high ponytail, those dark waves cascading to her shoulders. Her peacoat revealed a low-cut top that exposed a delicious slice of cleavage, and guaranteed Chelsea would be wearing some scorchingly hot, panty-melting number underneath. Her lips were pure carmine, and the smoky eyes glancing Kyle's way had her soaked on the spot.

"Do you need to use the bathroom or anything, or should we get going?" Ky asked, her legs tensing as if she needed to jog, or bolt, or something.

Chelsea's lips curled into a grin. "I'm all good if you are, sugar."

That fucking nickname. It *did* things to her every time Chelsea purred the words out.

"Let me grab my keys and wallet," Ky said, taking the excuse to bolt up her steps. She grabbed the necessary items from the kitchen table and took a moment to let out a long, slow exhale. No buffers tonight—just her and Chelsea in a place guaranteed to get her hot.

Why had she agreed to this, again?

Right, because she couldn't say no to Chelsea Moore, even if her heart might end up battered by the end of this.

This wasn't a date. Just two friends checking out a BDSM club together.

She failed to even convince herself at this point.

Kyle jogged down the steps again, a little breathless as she reached the bottom step to see Chelsea still there, leaning against the doorframe and looking like total sin. Kyle would kneel and worship at her altar any day of the week.

"Let's get going," Chelsea said, tapping her finger on the door before she took the first step out. Kyle locked up behind her and they set off.

The winter breezes carried the scents of gravel and oil, sharp and stinging. Kyle jammed her hands in the pockets of her leather, trying not to let the cold seep through. Chelsea strode next to her, the heels of her boots clicking on the asphalt. The Red Door was a seven-minute walk from Kyle's place, so they'd agreed to meet at her door. Which meant if any drinking happened, Chelsea would be crashing at her place tonight. The thought was dizzying.

"Have you been anywhere like this before?" Kyle asked, curiosity getting the better of her.

Chels pursed her lips, staring off at the street

ahead. "Never had the chance. When I started getting interested and brought the idea up to my ex, he always made me feel like some sick freak about it. Clearly, the guy couldn't have his masculinity threatened by a woman trying to top him."

Her heart thudded at hearing Chelsea talk about anything so vulnerable. The woman turned slick, sarcastic, and sensual at a moment's notice, but rarely did she let her guard down. Kyle waited for those few moments when Chelsea's eyes softened like the hazy glow of a camera filter.

"Well, jury's already out that your ex-husband was a dick," Kyle responded. From everything she'd heard from Aubrey and the little Chelsea confessed, Noah had been a selfish, dismissive asshole when Chelsea deserved so much better. "No partner should make you feel like shit about your sexuality and what you want to explore."

"Well, people can't all be unjudgmental sweethearts like you, Ky," Chelsea drawled with a wink. "What about you? Is this your first foray?"

Kyle lifted her brows and passed her a look. "Do you honestly think the woman who's terrified to talk to chicks at bars is going to have the stones to go to a BDSM club by her lonesome? Chances are, I'll just get a different flavor of rejections tonight."

"Are you kidding me?" Chelsea proclaimed. "You're like a Domme's wet dream. I bet you'll get scooped up in seconds."

Kyle's throat tightened. As if that stood a chance at happening. No one wanted the plain girl with the thick thighs and no rack. Mom pounded the sentiment home early on, disappointed by her daughter's lack of genetic inheritance. As the years went by, those lessons stacked one on top of the other in the form of crushes that went unrequited and countless, countless rejections. She'd seen the way women stared at Aubrey for years, and just once, she wished someone looked at her with the same desire in their eyes.

"Yeah, my track record pretty much assures that's not going to happen," Kyle responded, trying to sound unaffected.

Chelsea lifted a brow. "Says the woman who's goddamn gorgeous. Seriously, sugar. For every negative thing you say about yourself, I'm going to steal something sweet from your pantry until your chocolate stash is down to nothing."

A flush rose to Kyle's cheeks. She should be able to accept compliments, but every time anyone flirted or offered one, the words didn't warm her chest.

They were lone riders against an army of self-loathing she couldn't hope to defeat.

Kyle rubbed her hands along her sleeves, as if the motion could shed the prickle of vulnerability and discomfort that mingled with yearning every time Chelsea told her she was beautiful, something that happened more and more often.

"I'm going to have to go overboard stocking my pantry then," Kyle offered a grin, glancing to the end of the street where the neon-red lights spelled out the Red Door. Her heartbeat quickened as Chelsea nudged against her, all of those casual touches scorching her from the inside out.

A few folks loitered outside the brick building smoking cigarettes, and the bright red painted doors stood out less than a block away from where they were walking. The thump, thump, thump of her sneakers on the concrete comforted Kyle even as she waded into foreign territory. Somehow, facing all this newness with a bold, vibrant, and fearless woman like Chelsea caused the icy anxieties to melt around the edges.

Her biggest worry revolved around walking in and watching Chelsea get snatched up in moments by some muscular guy with a Crest-commercial smile while she sat at the bar alone, checking her phone and pretending she wasn't agonizing over sitting by herself. She was a big girl. She could do this.

Kyle strode to the door first and grabbed the handle, opening it wide. "After you, Chels. Knock 'em dead."

Chelsea swept inside, but a moment later she reached back to grab Kyle's hand, tugging her forward. The simple touch between them was raw electricity, and even after they'd stepped a couple of paces in, Chelsea didn't let go. Kyle's head dizzied from the sheer force of her attraction to this woman, a wild chemistry she'd never experienced before, not even with her handful of girlfriends over the years.

Chelsea came to a halt, and Kyle almost slammed into her back.

The Red Door was in full swing tonight, crimson lights slathering every surface in this sensual vibe. The décor themes were red and black, from the leather couches stationed throughout to the smooth polished bars on either side of the room. Three stages took up the center with plenty of comfortable seating around them, and the back of the bar held a dance floor as well as at least three closed doors on either side, probably leading to private playrooms.

Kyle chewed on her lip. Damn. Her gaze drifted

to the stages. One held a St. Andrew's Cross where a female submissive was getting tied up there by her Dom for the beginning of the exhibition. Kyle soaked in the sights, her body tingling and growing flush at the idea of what would take place on those stages.

At another platform, a Dominant prepared for a shibari exhibition. His sub knelt with his head down, dressed only in tight leather shorts that may as well have been underwear. Even still, the guy seemed at ease up there. What ensnared Kyle though was watching the Dom begin binding his submissive in rope, his hands moving with calm confidence.

Holy fuck.

She'd read some BDSM romance before and watched a few movies, but she hadn't been sure if this would be the scene for her until walking through these doors. Everything about this place sparked her libido more than she ever thought it would.

"Want to go grab a drink?" Chels asked, coming to her senses first.

Kyle bobbed her head in a nod, not trusting her mouth to do much more than stammer. Together, they wove their way over to the bar on the far right. She realized with a start Chelsea hadn't let go of her hand. Not like she'd dare pull away either. Kyle savored every one of these moments, knowing they'd have to tide her over for far longer when some available hot guy scooped up Chelsea while Kyle was left by her lonesome.

They took their seats, and Chelsea dropped her hand to begin unbuttoning her peacoat. The red shirt she wore was skintight with corset lacing down the front, and her black pants highlighted the gorgeous thighs Kyle hadn't been able to get off her mind since amateur burlesque night. She pulled her gaze away before she got caught drooling, because hell, the woman looked divine and smelled even better.

The moment the bartender came over, Chelsea ordered a glass of port and a gin and tonic and paid. Kyle's brows drew together as Chelsea glanced at her, the smile reflecting in those dark, gleaming eyes.

"Unless you were planning on ordering some other drink?" Chelsea crooked her brow.

Kyle fixed her with a look. "I'm not that predictable."

"Oh, but sugar, you are," Chelsea responded, her grin widening.

Kyle flipped her a middle finger even as she smiled in return. "I'm getting the next round."

Chelsea shook her head as the bartender swung over with her port. "Tonight's on me. You're the first person who's enabled this rather than making me feel like a freak, and that means something. Besides, if I don't get your drinks, then you'll get swept off your feet by some beautiful Domme, and I'll be sitting here by myself."

Kyle shook her head, letting out a laugh. "You realize I had the exact same fear, right? But out of the two of us, you're the one who's confident, stupidly hot, and looks like she stepped out of *Vogue*. I showed up in jeans and a button-down, for fuck's sake."

Chelsea took a sip from her port, the rich color mingling with the hue of her lips. "Like I'd let anyone sweep me off my feet. You've got to know me well enough by now to realize I'd be the one doing the sweeping."

God, yeah she would. From the moment they'd started hanging out, Chels sat behind the steering wheel, and Kyle adored the take-charge attitude. The woman didn't leave room for doubts to linger about whether she wanted to spend time together. The only thing Kyle had gotten tangled up in were the other feelings that jumped along for the ride: the mind-searing lust and the way her heart swelled every time she caught the woman's lingering glances, like this might not be one-sided.

The bartender returned, and Kyle took the first

sip of her gin and tonic. Both of the scenes had finished setup, and the Dom began his rope demonstration on his submissive. The low pulse of the music, the pleasant temperature, and the sensual lighting made the scene even hotter as she settled back, her elbows against the bar. Plenty of folks gathered onto the comfortable lounge seating, some sitting together, and one chick perched on another's lap. A guy knelt on the ground beside a woman who was dressed in a leather bustier and slim black pants, leaning against the red cushion.

The different dynamics fascinated her, and she couldn't help but soak everything in. She snuck a glance in Chelsea's direction. The woman's crimson lips were open as if she'd taken a soft puff of a breath and forgotten to close her mouth, and her eyes were lush with curiosity as she devoured every detail like she couldn't get enough.

Kyle switched her gaze back to the scene, watching the Dom begin to wrap those neat lines around the sub. She heard the creak of the stool next to her, and Chelsea's thigh brushed against hers. The tension in the room grew palpable as fevered gazes watched the demonstration onstage, the sub blissfully surrendering to the Dom's competent movements. She didn't need to glance to her right to feel the scorch of Chelsea's eyes on her this time.

The flush crawled up her neck from the awareness of all the woman's intensity fixated on her. Fuck, it was heady.

Even though Chelsea was straight, Kyle had tripped headfirst into falling for her, despite the hazards to her heart.

A woman took a seat next to her, tall and femme with a grace to her movements like she meant to be everywhere she landed. Her blonde hair was a shade probably termed ice, and her sharp nose fit with her defined lips all too well. She ordered a drink from the bartender and reached over, brushing her hand along Kyle's arm.

"Hey, I've got your next drink, okay?" the woman didn't quite ask with her tone but commanded instead.

Kyle's eyes widened. Anyone buying her a drink was a rare, rare occurrence. The blonde had shoulder-length hair and eyes like glaciers, and she wore a brown leather shirt and soft green pants. Way too attractive to be chatting her up.

"You look lost, sweetheart," the woman said, her lips curving in a grin. "First time here?"

Kyle offered a smile in response. "Is it that obvious? I bet my lack of leather and black sold me out."

"Maybe a little," the woman responded. "But it's more the sweet wide-eyed way you're taking everything in."

The bar stool rustled next to her. "I'll be right back," Chelsea said, tipping two fingers in her direction. "Bathroom."

A moment later, she rushed off, leaving Kyle alone. The blonde's grin widened, interest clear all over her gaze.

Goddamn.

CHAPTER EIGHT

CHELSEA STEPPED INTO THE WOMEN'S bathroom and sucked in a sharp breath.

She clutched the porcelain sink and stared into the mirror, grateful the three stalls behind her were empty. Everyone else was too focused on the scene taking place onstage to step away, but she'd needed to.

The cold from the sink seared into her palms, not calming the throbbing flame within her that had pushed her to bolt from the scene in the first place. Kyle might not see her own worth, but she was a once-in-a-lifetime sort of woman, and someone would snatch her up.

And tonight, she'd hoped—wondered if she'd summon the nerve to cross the line between them.

To satiate the curiosities that had begun to brim during every hangout and each meeting. Even with the gorgeous visuals on display, Chelsea didn't find herself wanting to jump into a scene with any random tonight.

No, only one person had been on her mind.

The fucking stunner who'd gotten pounced on by some savvy Domme who was probably comfortable with her sexuality and not questioning it. Kyle deserved someone like that. Someone far more stable than someone freshly out of a divorce and considering batting for both teams, her head tangled into such a mess that she couldn't even commit to a concert six months from now, let alone acknowledge maybe she wasn't as heterosexual as she'd once believed.

And yet, the idea of the woman at the bar claiming those soft lips, of taking Kyle home, stripping her down, and exploring every inch of that luscious body burned Chelsea up inside. She turned on the faucet to splash some ice water on her palms and her arms, needing to calm the fuck down before she let her jealousy turn her into an asshole.

Chelsea sucked in a sharp breath. What was her game plan?

Hell if she knew.

She took another breath to calm herself down. Chelsea would go out there and finish her glass. If Kyle had gone off with the hottie trying to pick her up, she'd let the woman be happy and just go introduce herself to some new folks. She could do this.

With that decision made, she shut off the faucet and pushed herself up to head back onto the main floor.

Chelsea stepped out, her gaze zeroing in on Kyle, who clutched the stool she sat on as the blonde leaned in to whisper something in her ear. Kyle grinned and ducked her head, the shy move so damn endearing she wanted to scream. Somehow in just a few weeks, the woman had managed to imprint on Chelsea more than she thought possible. The other scene on the platform with the St. Andrew's Cross started as a Dom began to practice swings with a flogger, the swish, swish, swish echoing in the air.

The sub was bound against the St. Andrew's Cross, biting her lip in anticipation. The sheen of desire in her eyes distracted Chelsea for a moment, reminding her of why they'd arrived here in the first place. Chelsea glanced up, and Kyle's eyes met hers from across the room. Her pulse sped, and she could imagine this woman spread out before her, blissed out like the tied-up sub.

She was a goner. Chelsea crossed the room, barely registering her footsteps as she made her way back to Kyle. The moans of the submissive and the smack of the flogger echoed through the room, the crowd quieting to a murmur. As she came closer, Ky turned toward the blonde Domme and offered a sweet grin, one that twisted Chelsea's insides to pieces.

She just needed to grab her drink and her purse to give Ky space with her new lady friend. She could do this.

Chelsea returned to her stool, but right as she settled into it, reaching for the wine she'd abandoned, the blonde Domme stood. The woman whispered something in Kyle's ear that made a beautiful flush spread on those cheeks, and then the blonde strode over toward the couches, closer to the exhibition.

Chelsea took a sip from her port, confusion trickling in amongst all the tangle of emotions she hadn't begun to card out yet. The dark, tart liquid calmed her, and she leaned in closer to Kyle. Even though part of her wanted to remain in the dark, she couldn't help her curiosity.

"Are the two of you going to meet up later?" she asked, the question coming out huskier than intended.

Kyle gripped her empty gin and tonic, sipping at the remainder that was only ice at this point. "Nope. Don't get me wrong, the woman's gorgeous and this whole getting hit on thing is totally foreign for me. But I remember agreeing to come check out the Red Door with you, not rush off with the first person who bats her lashes at me."

The heat flaring through Chelsea's chest sucked the remaining oxygen from her lungs. This goddamn woman. She'd never met another soul as selfless and loyal, which reaffirmed the attraction flaring between them from the moment they'd begun hanging out one-on-one.

"Looks like you could use a refill," Chelsea said, spinning around to face the bartender. "Another gin and tonic, please," she ordered before Ky got the chance to jump in.

Kyle's lips quirked in another one of those genuine heart-melting smiles. The woman brought out every ounce of possessiveness and protectiveness in her, even though she could barely summon the courage to say a damn thing.

Chelsea always figured if she'd ever realized she was gay, bi, or pan, it'd be a no-brainer to come out. After all, her sister paved the way with loud arguments and an aggressive stance, and she hadn't been excommunicated from the family.

Yet, every time Chelsea thought about the prospect, all she could see was the tight-lipped way her dad got around Aubs. How their relationship irrevocably changed. She'd already been a disappointment with her short-lived marriage and divorce. Adding more to the burn pile…. She didn't know if she could handle the heat.

The bartender passed her the gin and tonic, which she slid over to Ky. "Here you go, sugar. I've got your drinks tonight, remember?" She couldn't help the possessive words dripping from her tongue, or the unique pleasure that coiled in her chest as Ky's cheeks colored, her hazel eyes so earnest it cracked something inside of her.

"Thanks, Chels," she murmured, taking a sip.

"Thank you," Chelsea insisted. "Being able to watch what a scene might look like and get the balls to step inside the club was huge for me."

"Even if you don't get to sweep some hot guy off of his feet?" Kyle asked, a hint of tension in her question.

She wanted to correct her so badly, but those words stuck in her throat. Chelsea gave her the side eye instead. "Falling into a fling with a hot guy got me into a miserable marriage and a divorce, so no thank you. I'm just here to scope out the club with you tonight."

"Sounds perfect to me," Kyle responded, her shoulders relaxing in response. Chelsea's heart thudded a little harder. Fuck, she wanted to close the space between them and capture those cherry lips to see what the woman tasted like. Kyle glanced at her, her gaze sweeping to Chelsea's shoulders. "Your traps look really tight."

Chelsea pursed her lips. "Want to check?" she asked, exposing her shoulder. Not like she wasn't dying to have those hands on her bare skin.

Kyle leaned over and settled her hands along the muscle. The second she began to knead into them, Chelsea didn't bother restraining her moan. She couldn't help but watch the way Kyle's gaze flared with heat at the noise and how her grip tightened just a little more.

"Yeah, they're like cords, Chels," Kyle murmured, continuing to work on her shoulder.

Each knead of her fingers sent a thrill coursing through her that pooled in her core. Chelsea squeezed her thighs a little tighter together.

"Let me check the other side," Kyle said.

Chelsea tipped back the rest of her port. She would need another drink or three to survive tonight.

FIVE GLASSES of wine in and Chelsea was flying high.

She hadn't planned on drinking so much, but after watching three more women approach Kyle, who politely turned each of them down, Chelsea wanted to drag the woman out of here and either make out with her or cry in sexual frustration. She wasn't sure which way she swung, but the longer they remained here, the more she wanted to rip Kyle's clothes off. She might've even gotten drunk so she could crash at Kyle's place. Might have. She wouldn't admit to that one though.

Not like she could focus on Kyle with this stupid guy breathing down her neck.

Of course, the one person to approach her tonight was an arrogant Dom who made her fingers itch to deliver a one-two punch.

The guy smelled like he'd drowned himself in Nautica Voyage, which mixed horribly with the leather pants and sweat combo he toted along with him. The man was all muscles and annoyance, the exact sort of fucker she'd been looking to avoid at the usual bars. She tended to draw frat guys and assholes in like ants to sugar, and she wanted to know how to turn the shitty ability off.

Kyle got quieter the moment he sat next to them, and Chelsea just wanted to scream that she had no interest in this jackwad.

"How do you know you wouldn't like switching if you've never tried being a submissive?" the guy asked in a rich voice attempting cocky even though it came out more like a whine.

Chelsea pursed her lips, her nose wrinkling on instinct. "Just like you know you wouldn't want me shoving an eight-inch dildo up your virgin ass," she shot back. She couldn't tell for sure, but her instincts declared he was the sort who clung to his fragile masculinity like it was a baby blanket, using the title of Dom to get domineering with women, not dominant.

World of fucking difference.

He rolled his eyes. "That's ridiculous. Come on—you're clearly new here. Being close-minded isn't going to unlock your inner desires."

Chelsea fought back her gag. Did he think women got off on this? With the amount she had to drink, her filter had been stripped way down, and she was getting sick of any remaining distance or disruptions between her and Kyle.

"My inner desire is for you to leave me and this gorgeous woman alone, and no, she's not interested either," Chelsea shot back, loud enough to draw a few glances. "So you can either fuck right off, or we'll happily vacate."

The guy glowered at her, a flush rising from his neck to his face. When he rose, his shoulders twitched for a moment like he might try to take a swing at her. Chelsea steeled herself for the potential scrap, ready to do a whole lot more than chew him out. The room spun for a moment, and she gripped tight to the counter.

"No one's going to want a chick like you," he spat.

"Please—she'd find someone in a heartbeat," Kyle said, jumping to her defense.

When she glanced over, the woman almost stood out of her seat, her hands balled into fists. Chelsea couldn't help but reach over and run her fingers along those tensed fists. All of her emotions that she'd been trying to wrestle back all evening bubbled to the surface.

"Are you finished with your drink?" Chelsea asked, glancing to the empty gin and tonic on the bar counter. Hers only had a final sip left, which she didn't need to bother with. "Let's get out of here."

Kyle nodded, her fingers untensing, even though her shoulders remained squared. Fuck, Chelsea just wanted to collapse on her solid frame. Her vision turned hazy for a moment, like the woman had a real-life halo around her. So she was a little drunk. Sue her.

Chelsea looped her arm through Kyle's and tugged, dragging them in the direction of the door. The contact made her feel fuzzy, a warmth bubbling inside her that carried through even as they stepped out the door and into the brisk winter night. She swayed while she walked, and Ky's grip on her tightened until the woman walked with her arm wrapped around Chelsea's waist. Her core throbbed at the stable touch and at the way her body kept bumping and sliding against Kyle's on the walk back.

She caught a whiff of the brown-sugar-and-cinnamon scent that was pure Kyle Walker, and she couldn't restrain her moan. She wanted to lick this woman from head to toe. Ky's eyes widened at the sound, and her tongue darted out to wet her lips. The moonlight turned her auburn hair a purplish hue and highlighted her fine bone structure, from her pointed nose to her well-defined lips that Chelsea couldn't stop staring at.

"So, was the Red Door everything you thought it would be?" Ky asked, averting her gaze every time Chelsea stared her way.

"Mmm," Chelsea murmured, her head spinning a little with the motion as they continued to make their way to Ky's apartment. "The exhibitions were hot, and they got my rusty gears turning. I could've done without the constant interruptions though. Fucking forbid we get any time together."

Kyle snorted, her eyes crinkling at the edges. "Doll, you're tanked, aren't you?"

Chelsea cast her a pointed look. "What gave you that idea?"

"Beyond the fact that I watched you toss back five glasses of wine, your lack of volume control's a pretty good indicator." Kyle grinned, amusement dancing on her features. "Don't worry," she murmured. "It's cute."

"'M not drunk," Chelsea muttered, tugging on the end of her ponytail.

"Sure, you're not," Kyle responded. "Either way, we're going to get you an aspirin and some water before you crash out tonight."

Chelsea nestled in a little closer to Ky, her lips

brushing against her neck. The sharp intake of Kyle's breath made her pussy throb with desire. This woman felt like warm silk, and she was dying to taste her. The arm Kyle wrapped around her waist tightened a little bit, and the tension between them grew thicker.

Up ahead, Kyle's apartment came into view at the end of the block, one of the many bricked beauties lining Spring Garden. In such a short time, this place had become so familiar to Chelsea, just like the woman who lived there. She swayed a bit on her feet as they came closer, and Kyle's grip around her waist tightened. The way she pressed against Chelsea's body made her swoon.

"Careful. Don't want you tottering into traffic, Chels," Kyle said, remaining steady and solid even when her world spun. They came closer to her apartment where the black door beckoned. The warmth of this woman and the strong flare of protectiveness muddled Chelsea's head, mixing with Kyle's sweet, sugary scent of her that was so damn delicious.

Chelsea pivoted to turn toward Kyle, whose arm was still wrapped around her waist. Like this, her lips were mere inches away. Kyle glanced up, and the look in those hazel eyes undid some knot inside her. The fears that seemed insurmountable earlier faded away while captured in her soft, yearning gaze. Chelsea slid her fingers through Kyle's hair until she clutched her by the nape, and she closed the distance between them.

The moment her lips caressed Kyle's, she let out an unrestrained moan. They were softer than she'd imagined, the sweep of their mouths pressing together sending jolts of electricity rippling up and down her spine. Kyle's hands settled at her waist, her grip tightening in a way that made Chelsea's core throb. As the kiss deepened, she swept her tongue in, the crisp taste of gin and lime sparking her synapses to life. Chelsea stepped forward, Kyle moving with her to take one step and then another until Kyle's back thudded against the wall.

Chelsea didn't loosen her grip on Kyle's nape, adoring how the woman sank against her while she ravaged her mouth. Their kisses grew fevered, all tongue and teeth and heat. The wintry breeze swirled around them, but the cold couldn't pierce through the bubble of unrepentant desire driving her to the point of desperation.

Everything she'd been holding back was unleashed as she crushed her lips against Kyle's, capturing her mouth until they both gasped for air. She'd been burning for this woman for weeks, from every adorable, heart-melting smile to the way she combed her fingers through her hair when she got nervous or embarrassed. She tasted so damn sweet. Chelsea drove her tongue in until she coaxed out Kyle's moans against her mouth, lapping up every one of them.

She didn't want anything soft with this woman—no, she wanted to possess, to devour. Kyle brought out a savage side of her she'd never experienced and one she didn't want to cage. She thrust her leg between Kyle's, crowding her against the wall as she claimed her lips over and over again.

They finally broke apart for breath, and her mind swirled. Kyle's hands still rested on her hips, and their shoulders heaved up and down as they gasped in the cold November air. Chelsea stood there in silence for a moment, trying to make her surroundings stop spinning. All she could focus on was Kyle's swollen lips and the blush lighting her beautiful cheeks.

"You okay, Chels?" Kyle asked, bringing her palm up to cup her cheek.

Chelsea's tongue traced her lips. "I'm not going to lie—I want to devour every inch of you, sugar. But with the way the whole... everything... is spinning, that's probably not in the cards tonight."

Kyle ducked her head, her grin brightening as she slipped her arm around Chelsea's waist again. "Let's get you upstairs and into bed, doll."

"I'll happily slip into bed with you." The words flew from her lips before she could rein them back.

Kyle shook her head, even though she still smiled. "Come on. I'll even tuck you in." Kyle started guiding them toward the door, and as the effects of the wine settled in, Chelsea's limbs felt detached, like she barely had control over them.

"Rain check then," Chelsea murmured, leaning in to nip at Kyle's earlobe.

"Lord have mercy," Kyle swore under her breath as she fumbled with her keys to get her door unlocked.

Chelsea's eyes began to flicker as they headed up the staircase, her vision fading in and out to black.

The last thing she remembered before she passed out was a blanket settling over her and the press of Kyle's lips on her forehead.

CHAPTER NINE

"Thanks for helping with prep for next week, Ky," Aubs said as she continued to chop carrots. "The last thing I want to do is try to slam in all this work while I'm getting ready for family Thanksgiving."

Kyle washed another potato under the water and began peeling. In the past they held their Friendsgiving at whoever's space was bigger, but now that Sky and Mia had a gorgeous house they were renting and Selina and Aubs had moved into their townhouse together, they'd decided to take turns hosting. Kyle didn't want to cram folks into her apartment, so she just offered prep-work assistance where she could.

"Thanksgiving will be here in a blink," Kyle

murmured. Normally, she didn't give a damn about Thanksgiving with her family because the small affair turned strained between her and her mother most of the time. She showed up, ate fast, and evacuated as quickly as possible.

This year, however, Chelsea would be coming over the next day. *"Black Friday—Rain check?"* was the text Kyle had gotten the day after they'd gone to the club, and she hadn't been able to think about anything else. After the way they'd locked lips outside of her house, all Kyle could focus on was their kiss.

She'd never in her life received a kiss like that, one that eradicated all thought from her brain. Even though Chelsea had been plastered, she'd taken control with ease, and Kyle never felt safer than when she melted into Chelsea's grip. Too often, she worried if she gave enough tongue, if she should be more aggressive, or if she disappointed the other person.

Not with Chelsea. All she could think about was more, more, more, a desperate need flaring within her that had yet to be quenched. The woman who'd only ever been straight kissed with a fire Kyle hadn't expected, and God, the memory made her heart take a leap she couldn't afford.

Awkward thoughts to be having about Aubrey's sister while in her kitchen. Ones Kyle knew she should feel guilty over, if only she could even hope to smother the swarm of butterflies that had been unleashed in her chest.

"You're going to be bringing dessert, right?" Aubs asked, finishing her carrot chopping with a flourish. "Do we get to make requests?"

"Hell no," Kyle responded, a grin rising to her lips. Mostly because she'd promised Chelsea a reprisal of the chocolate cherry cupcakes she'd made for her before. "You want choices, then you buy from a bakery."

"Your stuff's better than most of the bakeries around here," Aubs responded, flashing her one of those devil-may-care grins. "I'll take whatever I can get, as long as it's not coconut."

Kyle shook her head. "I know you and your life-long hatred of all things coconut better than that, trust me. I wouldn't risk the wrath."

"Did you want to go to any bars on Black Friday? I can wingman for you," Aubs offered, casting her a genuine glance. "I feel like I've been a shitty friend recently. With my kickboxing classes being slammed and trying to juggle this whole being a girlfriend and having dual holiday obligations—it's been weird and a lot."

Kyle shook her head. "You haven't been shitty, Aubs. You're allowed to enjoy this, you know. I pushed you toward settling down in the first place."

Aubs looked up from the onion she'd started slicing, and Kyle couldn't tell if the onion or genuine emotion had made her eyes glassy. "Yeah, but you're the one who lives for this type of shit, and you deserve an awesome relationship more than anyone I know. I just feel guilty, like I left a soldier behind or something."

"If you start singing 'Love is a Battlefield,' I'm walking out," Kyle warned, even as her heart twisted. What Aubs described had been the exact way she'd been feeling—at least until Chelsea Moore flirted her way into her life.

"Damn onions," Aubs muttered, rubbing her forearm over her eyes. "I swear, I'm not bawling like a little bitch."

Kyle finished peeling another potato and placed a hand to her chest. "Wouldn't dare accuse you." If anything, she felt guiltier now. Unrequited lusting over Aubrey's younger sister was one thing, but Chelsea had kissed her—she'd *kissed* her, and not only that, she wanted more. And Kyle hadn't said a damn word to Aubrey. As supportive and generous as Aubs could be, the one person she tended to get irrational over was Chelsea.

"It's going to feel more like a family Thanksgiving than a friends one this year," Aubs grumbled, sweeping the chopped onions into the skillet on the stovetop as she cooked them down with the carrots. "Since Selina, Chelsea, and I will already be attending the family one two days earlier. So weird having my little sis there."

Kyle shrugged, trying to ignore the bubbles floating inside her at the mere mention of Chelsea. Fuck, she had it bad. "Yeah, but the offer probably means a lot to her right now. Dealing with the post-Noah fallout must suck, and you've even said she doesn't have a lot of friends."

Aubrey pursed her lips, her brows drawing together like she was mulling over something.

Kyle continued peeling potatoes, focusing on the work beneath her hands and not at Aubrey. She was a garbage liar to begin with, and if she met Aubrey's gaze, she'd probably start spewing enough random crap to get anyone suspicious.

"For someone getting out of a divorce, though, I figured I'd see her out a lot more. She's been busy, but she's been secretive too." Aubs continued moving the simmering carrots and onion around in the skillet as she mused aloud. "The only time she gets like this is if she's seeing someone. Chelsea's always kept her relationships quiet unless she's a hundred percent sure it's the real deal."

Kyle struggled to keep the flush from her cheeks. Were they seeing each other? Fuck, she didn't know anything beyond Chelsea making her life a million times better in the past few weeks. And Chelsea had kissed her. But that could mean anything, from satisfying curiosity to lasting forever.

"Would it be bad if she was seeing anyone?" Ky asked, her heart beating so loud Aubrey could probably hear every slam. She fought the weight in her voice, trying to keep it light and curious.

Aubs shrugged. "As long as he's not another douchebag like Noah. I'm hoping she's done with those sorts of guys. He never showed when she needed someone solid, and I always hated him for that. If she'd been truly happy, I could've found a way to deal with his meathead drivel, but on top of the lack of smarts, he was an asshole too."

"Or maybe she's just enjoying the single life," Ky said, finishing with the last potato in the bowl. Fuck, she needed something else to do with her hands.

Aubs cast her a direct look, one she felt. "Please.

I know my baby sister. If she's been hitting up the bars or sleeping around, she'd be loud and proud about it. We've both always been that way. The only time she clams up like this is if there are feelings involved."

Ky's pulse sped with a desperate hope she could barely stand. Chelsea had only been hanging out with her. Since the morning after the divorce party, they'd been glued at the hip, to the point that Chelsea came over on weeknights, playing her favorite Zelda game on her handheld while Kyle found a new recipe to bake, something random from Netflix playing in the background. The whole thing had gotten so domestic so fast, and the comfort made her heart spasm.

The time she spent with Chelsea Moore was everything she'd dreamed of from a relationship, and ever since that kiss, *that kiss*, she couldn't convince herself those hopes were impossible because Chelsea was straight.

She was something, all right, but no straight girl kissed like that—not even when she wanted to dip her toes in the pool.

"Well, hopefully you like this one better than the last" was all Kyle could push out, after far too much time had passed.

A knock pounded on the door, drawing the attention away from her. Oh, thank fuck.

A moment later, the door creaked open. "I'm here with your goddamned decorations, Aubs." Sky's voice echoed to the rafters of the place. "Mia's slaving away at home on some artsy idea she got on a whim, so she might be bringing other stuff with her on Saturday."

"We're in the kitchen," Aubs called, chasing her carrots and onions with a spatula.

Kyle washed her hands and wiped them down on a kitchen towel as she turned to see Sky walking through the archway toting a big box of decorations. Sky blew a lock of her pixie cut out of her face as she sauntered into the room.

"We used these last year, so I guess they can just be the traveling décor for whoever's hosting," Sky said, dropping the box on the table. She glanced at Ky and broke into a grin. "Holy shit, how long's it been since the three of us were hanging out? I'm getting some major old-school nostalgia."

Aubs let out a low whistle as she glanced between the two of them. "Way too long. I was telling Ky earlier what a crap friend I've been, and I think this confirms it. We need a regular night for the three of us. Girlfriends at home."

"Count me in," Kyle said, offering a soft smile. Her heart squeezed with relief at hearing Aubrey say that, but even as she did, the ever-present reminder weighed down on her. She didn't have anyone waiting at home for her, and some nights, the ache grew so intense she thought she might surrender to the coldness of her empty bed, to the arsenic-laced quiet sweeping through her house when she longed to hear murmurs.

Sky strode over and slung an arm around Kyle's shoulders, as if she'd sensed the turmoil in her mind. Kyle leaned in, accepting the affection. Aubrey formed the teeth of their friend group, and Sky stepped in with all warm hugs and encouragement. Kyle had always been the stable one who showed up, time and time again.

"We're not trying to flaunt our relationships," Sky murmured. "I promise. I want the same for you too, babe."

Kyle's eyes burned, but she kept the smile plastered on her face. "As long as you two aren't shoving me at any more randos in bars, I'm pretty sure I'll be good."

Aubrey brandished her spatula. "One of these days it'll work, though. I swear."

Sky arched a brow. "Are we talking about the

same Kyle Walker here? I'm pretty sure she's allergic to random hookups, and that's what's destined with the chicks you meet at a bar."

Kyle sniffed. "I can be adventurous."

"Adventurous like cliff diving or adventurous like wearing a pair of heels to the bar?" Aubs responded, an affectionate grin on her face.

Kyle flipped her the middle finger, even though her chest thudded with warmth. She'd missed this more than she'd realized.

Even still, she continued to flirt with fire.

She might not have a girlfriend, or someone to come home to every night, but she did have the promise from Chelsea Moore to rock her world on Black Friday.

And based on the subtle hints Chels dropped all week, there would be a whole lot more than kissing going on at this sleepover. She might be heading in for a disaster and she might end up shattered by the end of this, but she'd been living in fear for far too long. This was her first breath of adventure, and no matter the consequences, she'd seize it.

CHAPTER TEN

THANKSGIVING USED TO BE CHELSEA'S FAVORITE holiday, but this year, she looked forward to Black Friday far, far more.

After her drunken kisscapade with Kyle, Chelsea could've denied everything, and Kyle had given her the chance to.

But, hell, that kiss. Chelsea couldn't get it out of her mind if she tried, just like Kyle Walker appeared in her thoughts with a maddening frequency. So instead, she'd asked for the rain check, and ever since she'd gotten the balls to send the text, each day that drew the day closer had her nerves amping higher and higher.

She just needed to survive Thanksgiving dinner tonight. Aubs and Selina would be joining them soon, but since she was the single one this year, she'd headed over early to help Mom out with the casseroles. She finished pouring the mushroom sauce over top of the green-bean casserole and popped it in the oven, the rich scents causing her stomach to grumble. The stuffing was already bubbling. It was one of her favorites, with plenty of sage and dried cranberry.

She grabbed the potholder and pulled out the stuffing, the top a nice golden brown while the sides sizzled. God, she could eat a horse or a rhinoceros at this point.

Her phone buzzed, and she slipped it out to check—Kyle, though that wasn't a new occurrence. They texted each other from the moment they woke up to the good night texts when they went to bed— that is, when she wasn't crashing at Kyle's apartment. Better than her own hollowed-out place filled with empty spaces from her divorce.

We're starting dinner early, thank fucking Christ. Mom's warned me not to eat too much three times already.

Chelsea's gut tightened. No wonder Ky talked down about herself so often. Half of the things Kyle told her about her mother made Chelsea want to roll up to the Walker's house and punch the woman in the face. The Walker Christmas gathering would be a goddamn delight, especially if she had anything to drink.

The one Chelsea would attend as Kyle's fake girlfriend. The reality crashed down on her, souring in her stomach.

Chelsea shook it off and typed a response.

Please, you've got one of the hottest bodies I've ever seen. Eat as much as you want. In fact, if I show up tomorrow to find out you've starved yourself, I'll be forced to punish you.

She pursed her lips, her heart beating a little faster. The heat from the oven and the steaming dishes on the counter didn't compare to the combustion inside her body right now.

Hot. Why does that turn me on?

Kyle's response had Chelsea's lips curling as she shot back one more of her own.

Not the sexy kind of punishment either, so enjoy your Thanksgiving dinner. I'll be thinking of you all night.

She shoved her phone into her pocket, trying to ignore how her pulse roared like she had entered the Daytona 500. Her skin flushed at all the fantasies flooding through her at the idea of going to Ky's tomorrow. Neither of them acknowledged taking the next step, but the way their texts had grown sexier and sexier all week left little doubt in her mind that they were on the same page.

Mom bustled on in, snapping her out of her bubble. "You've got the last casserole in?" she asked, scanning from one end of the kitchen to the other.

Chelsea nodded. "Green bean is in, and I'm getting ready to carry the stuffing out to the dining room. We're all good here. No worries."

Mom passed her a grateful look. "You're the only reason I'm not spiraling out right now, sweetheart. Having your help today has been invaluable."

A knock pounded at the door.

Chelsea cast her a knowing look. "Must be Aubs and Selina, right on time. Think Dad will offer more than five sentences to Selina?"

Mom pursed her lips, a no-nonsense look on her face. "He better. We had a lengthy talk this week about what's appropriate, no matter his discomfort. It was more obvious at the last family function with the way he chattered Noah's ear off, so maybe this will be a bit easier."

Chelsea's stomach tightened. Even though Mom stepped to bat for Aubs, every single instance Dad froze up around her older sister or went straight to ignoring her carved Chelsea's gut to ribbons. In those moments, he'd always diverted all of the attention to her, and she'd lapped it up—sometimes just to keep more fights from breaking out in the family.

If she pursued anything real with Kyle, she'd have to tell him.

And then he'd look at her with those frostbitten eyes. The idea made her whole body revolt.

"I'm sure tonight will go great, Mom," Chels said, picking up the stuffing with oven gloves. "Why don't you get the door and I'll get this to the table."

Mom leaned in and kissed her on the side of her head. "Don't think I'm oblivious to all you do to keep the peace. Thank you, sweetheart." With that, she took off toward the front door while Chelsea headed in the direction of the Thanksgiving table.

In the Moore household, Thanksgiving had become a big tradition, and from her earliest years she remembered the massive feast that would take them weeks to go through. Tonight was no different. The turkey already sat steaming in the center of the table with Mom's golden tablecloth and plum candles artfully stationed around it. All of the place settings were finished, and Dad took his place at the head of the table, opening the bottles of shiraz and chardonnay.

The scents barraged her, making her nearly

drool, from the piping hot dinner rolls in the basket to the canned and from-scratch cranberry sauce. An array of other foods dominated the table, including a sweet-potato casserole, the stuffing she had placed beside it, corn, brown-sugar carrots, and more mashed potatoes than they could eat in a year.

"Is the whole thing for me?" Dad asked, his eyes crinkling around the edges.

"Like you could finish all this stuffing," Chelsea said, arranging the dish along with the others. The gravy looked amazing, and she couldn't wait to pour the fragrant liquid over everything on her plate, a habit that never failed to gross out Aubrey.

Her phone buzzed—guaranteed it was Kyle sending another text. Even though she wanted to, Chelsea didn't pull her phone out to check. Guilt flooded through her, like she was playing a role here with her father, masquerading around as his perfect heterosexual daughter.

If he knew the truth about what she had planned for tomorrow, he wouldn't be looking at her with those affectionate smiles any longer. Bile rose in her throat.

The oven timer beeped, saving her from trying to fake anything else. "I'll go grab the last casserole, and then we're good to go."

"Thanks, *mija*," he said, his thick accent a reminder of home, of their family.

Her heart pounded faster at everything she might lose if she indulged in these emotions flaring up every time she was around Kyle. She quickened her steps to the kitchen and snagged the green-bean casserole, turning the oven off in the process. Enough time to suck in a sharp breath and attempt to clear her head. By the time she re-entered the dining room, Mom already brought Aubs and Selina in, and they'd taken their seats at the table. Chelsea dropped the casserole off in the one clear spot left on the tabletop and then headed to claim her seat.

"Hey, sis," she said and swung by to offer Aubs a hug along her way. "Hey, Selina." Once she gave both of them a tight squeeze, she settled into place by Dad. Mom arranged them that way for a reason. They didn't have the buffer of Noah this year to distract Dad and Aubs from fighting, so instead of doing what Mom had hoped, Dad's raincloud silence amplified in the absence.

"The food looks great, guys," Selina offered, trying to get the conversation rolling.

"I'm betting you didn't let Dad near the kitchen," Aubs said, casting a glance between Mom and Dad. While Mom grinned in amusement, their father hadn't stopped looking at Selina like an intruder had arrived.

"Why don't you say grace, Alejandro," Mom said, a warning in her tone he couldn't miss.

He coughed and then nodded, interlacing his fingers and bowing his head as he launched into the grace before meals. *"Gracias a Dios por la comida,"* he began, and the rest of his prayer turned into a familiar melody to her ears.

Her fingers itched to dive into the food—chances were, eating would resolve half of this tension, since no one could say much with their mouth full. She was grateful no one shone a spotlight on the absence at the table this year, especially because Noah had been with her for three Thanksgivings, and this marked her first without him.

As much as the 'good riddance' crept to her tongue, the approach of the holidays hit a little harder being single this time around. Knowing that at Christmas there'd be no private exchange of gifts at home in the morning before they headed off to the family festivities and she'd be going back to wading through the big Christmas dinner by her lonesome—all of it sliced under her skin. She was haunted by invisible losses she hadn't anticipated.

The one shining light through this had been her friendship, or whatever was going on, with Kyle.

Yet that was also the biggest challenge she grappled with as well.

"All right, let's dig in," Mom said once Dad finished his prayers.

Chelsea didn't need to be told twice. She reached out and started shoveling stuffing onto her plate, followed with a hefty helping of glistening corn. Within minutes, her plate filled up with buttered rolls, slabs of turkey, mounds of mashed potatoes, and all of the good stuff she couldn't wait to mix together and deliver to her mouth. To top off her feast, she took the gravy and started drizzling it over any surface she could find.

"Don't mind my sister, Selina," Aubs commented, her voice extra loud to project. "She was raised by a pack of rabid gravy-loving coyotes who eat like savages."

Selina snorted. "Not everyone likes to chop their food into militant bits and keep it wholly separated, sunshine."

"Why would I taint my cranberry sauce with gravy?" Aubrey argued. "That can't taste good."

"Mmm, delicious," Chelsea said, projecting just as loud. She chewed on her food and made sure to smack her lips a bunch. Mom shook her head, an amused smile on her lips, and even Dad broke down a bit, his eyes crinkling like they'd all transported back in time to the years before Aubrey came out and Dad started treating her differently.

Selina smirked and dripped a small amount of gravy on her plate, then speared a cranberry with her fork and dipped it in. She brought the concoction to her lips, chewed thoughtfully, and then swallowed. "It's not the worst I've ever had."

Aubrey clutched at her chest, horror written all over her features. "You're no girlfriend of mine, eating monstrosities like that."

"Tough," Selina responded. "You're stuck with me."

Chelsea grinned, entertained by their antics. When she glanced across the table, her smile disappeared. Dad all but glowered in their direction, despite the promise he'd made Mom to do better this time around. He met her eyes and offered a half smile, the most he'd give right now.

"Have you been going out on dates, Chelsea?" Dad asked, his attempt at conversing on something that took away from his discomfort.

Aubs's expression darkened for a moment when he switched focus again, but her sister leapt in anyway. "I've been wondering the same thing. You've been pulling the elusive dance you only do when you've found someone you're interested in."

Chelsea nearly choked on the forkful of mashed potatoes and gravy. The truth... was a lot more complicated than she could ever voice right now. "I'm just going out to bars and stuff, trying to spend time with friends and enjoy being single."

"You know," Dad mentioned, drawing the tines of his fork along the plate. "I'm pretty sure Noah misses you."

Chelsea pursed her lips, delivering her father a flat-lidded stare. "More like you miss him. I'm pretty sure you two made a better couple than we did."

"No. He's mentioned coming back to the area around Christmas break. The boy just wants to see you again," Dad said, chewing on a piece of roll. "You know it's not too late to change your mind on the divorce. You still have a few months before it's official."

Chelsea's insides iced at his words. The picture they began to form caused her to brace herself. "Mentioned it? As in, you're keeping in contact with my ex-husband?" By some miracle, she maintained a level voice.

"Alejandro," Mom said, her voice sharpening. "You never told me you were talking to Noah."

"The boy reached out to me," Dad said, looking as unapologetic as ever. "*Mija*, you were so good together, and he wants to give the relationship another try. Don't you think it's worth listening to him?"

The idea of letting Noah back into her life repulsed her, but what smacked her in the face with an iron gauntlet was the fact her father had been talking to him behind her back this whole time.

"Dad, Noah's always been a piece of shit," Aubrey jumped in, coming to her defense like she always did. "Why the hell would you try to drag him back into her life? You know he never showed to all of the important things."

Chelsea swallowed, the Thanksgiving dinner sitting like a packed brick of ash in her stomach. The idea of Noah and her father being chummy after she'd divorced him struck her with the sort of betrayal she didn't tolerate. If that wasn't bad enough, attempting to convince her to give the relationship another try took the legs off of every ounce of support he'd offered when she broke the news.

Fuck, had Dad ever understood her at all? Or did they get along because she played the good kid to

Aubrey's rebellious side, the one trying to smooth things over and iron out any wrinkles in the family fabric?

Chelsea tasted bile, and her fingers began to tremble. She needed to get out of here—now. "You know, I think something I ate earlier is hitting me the wrong way," she murmured, pushing up from the table. "I'm going to call it an early night and try to sleep this off."

Loud voices sounded in the background, but Chelsea tuned them all out. She didn't want to hear Aubrey's defense or Mom try to reconcile everyone's flared tempers. She didn't want to hear a damn excuse from her dad's lips.

Chelsea grabbed her purse, shaking her head as Mom stepped into the foyer, holding her hand up like she might attempt to stop her. She forced a smile she didn't feel in the slightest, her fingertips numbed at the edges. "I'm just not feeling well," Chelsea insisted, even though they both could see past the lie.

Before anyone else could try to stop her, she stepped out the door and into the brisk November air where she belonged. The cold smacked against her skin, chilling her as much on the inside as on the outside. She managed to tug out her phone. Kyle had shot her one more text that said, *Sweet relief. I'm home.*

There was one place in the world Chelsea wanted to be right now.

She hopped in her car, started the ignition, and drove.

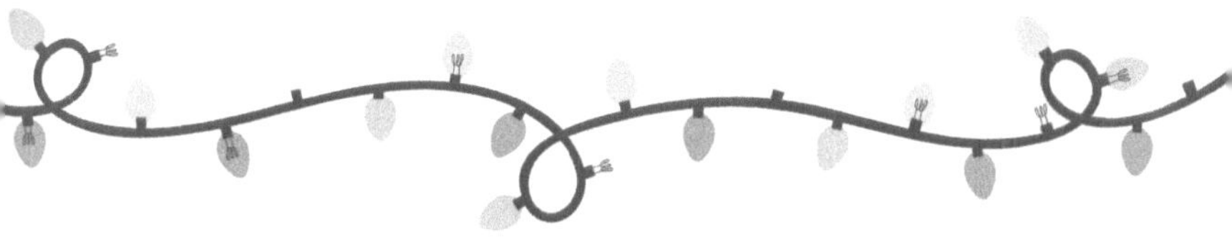

CHAPTER ELEVEN

Kyle pulled out a pear cider from her fridge, needing something stiff after the joy that had been family Thanksgiving. Her family dinner always started early, which meant she could scoot out just as quickly once the main meal ended. She'd spent most of the time catching up with Jake and avoiding the way Mom pursed her lips and dropped pinched comments as if they weren't more like detonated bombs. The breaking point had been when Dad mentioned packing some leftovers for her in the other room and Mom told him no because she thought Kyle was looking a bit chubby as of late.

Fucking sue her for having big hips.

The moment she heard that, she started getting

herself ready to go, but Jake told her to wait. He'd snuck back with containers of leftover mashed potatoes and stuffing, two things her mother would've left off her plate due to the ever-forbidden calories. Kyle had given him one big, wrenching hug before leaving without saying goodbye to her folks. She was so tired of the damage her mother caused every time she showed up.

Kyle leaned back in her couch and twisted the cap off. The cool, crisp liquid coursed down her throat, and she sank into the comfort of being home.

A knock pounded at her door.

Kyle's brows drew together. Who'd be visiting her on Thanksgiving evening while everyone hung out with their families? She placed her cider on the coffee table and slowly rose. Her left hand snuck into the pocket where she kept her knife, just in case, as she made her way down the steps to see who had arrived. She tugged the door open.

Chels stood at her doorstep, wearing her peacoat, a black dress, and heels, like she'd come from her own family dinner. The woman's dark waves were pulled back in a loose chignon, and like always, she looked fucking gorgeous, her defiant chin, smooth sepia skin, and expressive lips mesmerizing. Except

Kyle didn't miss the slight smear of redone mascara or the lingering redness around her eyes.

"Hey," Kyle murmured, cracking the door open wider. "What's wrong?"

Chelsea crossed over the threshold of the door, closing the space between them.

Kyle had barely nudged the door shut when Chelsea's lips crushed against hers. After spending the past week craving the taste of this woman, a moan slipped from her. That night it had been red wine she tasted, but this time she was offered a hint of cranberry and the sweet tang that was pure Chelsea Moore. She melted into the woman's grip around her hips as Chelsea steered her against the stairwell wall.

Kyle had never experienced anything like kissing this woman, a consuming desperation she wanted to surrender to every time. All thoughts vanished from her mind as she wrapped her arms around Chelsea's shoulders, her back pressed against the wall as their bodies crushed together. Her nipples pebbled as their chests brushed, separated by layers alone. Chelsea drove her tongue into Kyle's mouth with a fierceness that felt like possession, and she couldn't help but melt even more.

Chelsea's lips were velvet soft, and her mouth was scorching, mesmerizing. Her nails bit in past the flimsy fabric of Kyle's leggings as the woman gripped her harder, pinning her against the wall. The aggressive way Chelsea kissed, how she crowded into her space, made Kyle delirious with need—she'd never gotten this turned on from a kiss before. The way Chelsea chased every breath, consuming her mouth like she was starved, had Kyle's pussy throbbing. Her panties were soaked.

Chelsea pulled away for a gasping breath and that snapped Kyle out of the sudden reverie. She glanced up, and their eyes met. Kyle reached out to brush her thumb along Chelsea's cheekbone, close to the slight puffiness in her eyes.

"Well, that was one hell of a greeting," Kyle murmured, unable to help the giddy smile bubbling to the surface even as it warred with concern. Dinner must've gone awry for Chelsea to be showing up on her doorstep tonight. "Why don't we head upstairs? You look like you could use a drink, or something."

"Or something is right," Chelsea muttered. "Hell, I'm sorry for dropping in like this."

Kyle shook her head. "You never have to apologize for coming over, doll. I'm always happy to see you." Her lips still pulsed from the kiss, but she needed to get off this fast-paced freeway. She cared too damn much about Chels to let the woman drown in physical avoidance, no matter how good this felt.

Chelsea threaded her fingers through Kyle's, and she just about swooned. The contact before sent her senses into overdrive, but now that they'd kissed and the attraction wasn't one-sided? Holy hell.

"I left Thanksgiving dinner early—figured I'd take your cue of fashionably ducking the fuck out." Even with Chelsea's sarcastic tone, Kyle didn't miss the bitter tinge or the heavy weight there. Chelsea's phone buzzed in her coat pocket, and Kyle would place a bet Aubs was texting, wondering where her sister had gone.

Kyle squeezed Chelsea's hand as they reached the top of the steps, and she led them toward the kitchen. "I think I've got a few of the beers you left in my fridge if you want one."

"Yes, please," Chelsea responded.

Kyle reluctantly let go of her hand to grab a coffee porter from the fridge, crack the top, and pass it on over to Chelsea. "Didn't know I was a trendsetter. You tell me yours, and I'll tell you mine."

The corner of Chelsea's lip quirked as she

wound her way over to the couch where Kyle had been sitting. She flounced down and shrugged off her peacoat, dropping it over the arm of the couch before she kicked off her shoes to make herself comfortable. When Kyle took the seat right beside her, Chelsea leaned in against her. Kyle couldn't help but wind an arm around Chelsea's shoulders, bringing her as close as possible. The woman's hurt pulsed through the air, and Kyle hated that more than anything.

"I'll go first," Chelsea said with a trembling sigh that shuddered through her body. "My father's been talking to my ex-husband behind my back. He's convinced we're going to get back together or some delusional bullshit. It's bad enough how he treats Aubs and Selina, but I've been trying to keep him placated for years. I thought... Well, fuck, I thought the effort might mean something more than getting shoehorned into what's convenient for him." Bitterness exploded from her tongue, her dark eyes flashing with uncontained anger.

Chelsea never said it out loud, but her hurt pulsed through the air between them.

Kyle squeezed her a little tighter. The woman rarely opened up on anything deeper than surface, so Kyle understood just how much this meant. She leaned down and brushed her lips against the top of

Chelsea's head, like this close comfort was something normal between them.

"That's total crap. Noah's always been a dick, and your dad has no business talking to him," Kyle murmured. "I'm sorry you had to deal with his bull-shit on Thanksgiving."

Chelsea nuzzled in closer. "It just makes me wonder," she said, her voice growing whisper soft. "Why am I still trying to make him happy? Clearly, he doesn't give a damn about what I want." A tinge of fear lingered in her voice, and Kyle could under-stand why. Hell, if Chelsea's dad knew where she'd come running to, that the two of them kissed, he'd start treating her the way he did Aubrey. The thought twisted her stomach like a splash of bitters.

Chelsea reached over and tapped a finger on her chest, the pointed contact making her shiver. "So now you've got my reason for randomly showing up on your doorstep, but what was the tipping point that made you duck out early?"

Kyle swallowed hard. It was one thing internal-izing all the crap Mom spewed at her over the years, but saying the bile out loud in front of the woman she found herself devastatingly attracted to created a whole different hurdle. "I overheard my folks in the other room," she muttered. "Apparently I'm too fat to need leftovers. Guess it's a miracle I squeezed out the door without getting stuck."

Chelsea shot up, her brows drawing together. Her dark eyes blazed with anger, like unspent coals. "Fuck that woman," she spat. "You've got fantasy-inspiring hips, and every inch of you is beautiful. I hate that shit. I hate how she keeps tearing you apart over and over again."

Kyle shrugged, vulnerability washing over her. She'd grown so used to the scars getting picked open again that she just weathered the pain every time. "Clearly I lost the genetics lottery, that's all."

"Bullshit," Chelsea responded, turning to face her. She reached over to brush a few strands of hair behind Kyle's ear. "Do you know how much I've masturbated over the idea of fucking you this past week? How much I've fantasized about spreading you out on that bed and licking and sucking every inch of you? I've needed to recharge my vibrator almost nightly."

A whole-body flush swept through Kyle at the candid way Chelsea spoke, the sexual words dripping past her lips like promises. The woman made her want to bare everything, even though she normally fucked in the dark and tried to keep parts of her body hidden or obscured.

"Damn," Kyle said, licking her too-dry lips. "You have no idea how much you turn me on."

Chelsea shifted to swing her legs around until she was straddling her. She rested her arms on Kyle's shoulders, clasping her hands around them. Their lips were inches apart, and she couldn't avoid the intensity in Chelsea's liquid gaze. "So, you're telling me if I slide my fingers past your waistband and along your folds, I'll be able to feel the proof? I bet you taste like fucking candy."

Lord have mercy, this woman.

Chelsea leaned in, drawing her lips across Kyle's and sliding her tongue along the seam. Kyle opened to her, unable to resist this woman. This wasn't the same desperate, demanding kiss as the first two—instead, Chelsea seduced her with her lips in long, drawn-out strokes and the slow glide of their tongues. She could feel the inches still between them with a hunger that made her burn for them to be bared, skin to skin.

Chelsea's warm thighs trapped her on either side. Nothing thrilled Kyle more than being caged in by this woman. She'd take her however she could get her, and if that meant she was bound or begging, it didn't matter.

Chelsea pulled back to stare at her again. Kyle's

lips tingled in response to those caresses, her core throbbing for more, more, more.

"I want you," Chels murmured, her voice husky. "I could tell you a thousand times how beautiful you are, but I know none of those words will land. Let me show you."

"But you had such a garbage night," Kyle said, not wanting to come together just because their evenings were dumpster fires. If she were honest, Chelsea already staked a sober claim on her a week ago, but the excuses bubbled to her lips regardless.

Chelsea shook her head. "The second I came here, my night got exponentially better, and I plan on making it memorable. The only thing I need to know is: do you want this, sugar?"

Kyle licked her lips again, unable to help herself. She bobbed her head, her throat squeezing tight.

Chelsea shook her head. "Use your voice."

"Yeah," Kyle murmured, glancing away. "I want you so badly I can barely breathe, gorgeous."

Chelsea's lips curled into the sort of confident smile that bowled her over, a hunger lighting her features Kyle had a hard time believing. No one had ever looked at her like that before, like she was a work of art, or something beautiful enough to memorize.

"Then buckle up, sweetheart, because we're just getting started," Chelsea murmured, leaning in again. She didn't launch for Kyle's mouth this time—no, this time she swerved to the side and pressed her lips along Kyle's neck. The shiver running through her was pure electricity as Chelsea nipped and sucked her way down the column of her throat. Those deliberate ministrations felt so damn good.

She reached out, not sure where to put her hands or what to do against the onslaught of sensations this woman delivered. A moment later, Chelsea grabbed her by the wrists, pinning them back against the couch with one hand. The steel grip alone flipped her switch, but the way that possession made her mind shut off? She'd never experienced that before.

Chelsea leaned down further to lick along her collarbones, the puff of her breath sending a thrill through Kyle's spine. She'd grown so wet she'd need to wring out her underwear, and yet Chelsea continued to tease and caress her with her mouth. The tank top and sweats she wore bore down on her skin, as if the layers might smother her when she longed for skin-to-skin contact. She couldn't help but notice how Chelsea's black dress hiked up her thighs, exposing more and more smooth skin.

God, she wanted to just bury herself between

those strong legs and lick Chelsea's pussy until she screamed. Her desire for this woman had been scorching through her veins ever since the night of her divorce party where the idea of Chelsea as straight and unavailable grew muddled.

Chelsea pulled a hand back as she pushed herself up. Her fingers descended to the hem of Kyle's tank top.

Kyle bit her lip, vulnerability washing over her. "I'm all gross and bloated from dinner," she murmured. "You don't want to see what's under there."

Chelsea slid the strap of her tank top to her shoulder and bit Kyle's shoulder, her teeth sinking in with a vicious sting. Kyle's thighs squeezed tighter, the throb of her clit intensifying. "Next time you talk down about yourself, I'll bite harder," Chelsea warned, tenderness flashing in her eyes. "I very much want to see those gorgeous tits."

She reached down and brushed her fingertips across the tips of Kyle's nipples, pebbled and tight to the point that they protruded through the flimsy fabric. The sensation made her back arch as she bucked against Chelsea, who still had her caged between her thighs with her wrists pinned against the couch. Chelsea didn't stop teasing, her thumb brushing against her nipples until the layer of fabric became too much.

"Fine," Kyle burst out, unable to disguise the raw hunger in her voice. "Please take it off."

"See, sugar?" Chelsea said, leaning in to brush their lips together. "Progress."

The kiss was so sweet she gasped into it right as Chelsea began to slide the hem of her tank top up. She barely had the time to process as Chelsea broke the kiss and yanked her tank top up further. Chelsea released her wrists, and Kyle sat up an inch to help as the woman peeled the flimsy fabric off her and threw it to the floor. The urge to cover her tits swept in fierce, but before she could, Chelsea pinned one of her wrists again, bringing her other hand to circle around her breast.

"You're fucking stunning," Chelsea breathed. The normal shudder of nerves didn't have the chance to arrive, because a moment later, Chelsea dipped down and licked the tip of her nipple. Coherent thought zipped off at the nearest exit as a thrill climbed down her spine, pooling between her legs. Chelsea squeezed her breast and played with each of them, alternating back and forth until Kyle couldn't hold back her moans any longer. Chelsea's lips curled as she glanced at her.

"Bet you're fucking soaked for me, sweetheart," Chelsea murmured, her midnight eyes drenched with desire. The woman's throaty voice spun an intoxicating spell. She reached for Kyle's waistband and glanced up, a questioning look in her eyes.

Kyle couldn't help but bob her head to nod her permission. Remembering Chelsea's earlier statement, she forced a single word out. "Yes."

She'd never let anyone expose her like this, not under the light, but Chelsea was impossible to resist. The woman had her begging to obey every command and request.

Chelsea slid her waistband and panties down her legs, and Kyle shimmied her hips to try and help the fabric down further. The idea of the woman dropping between her thighs lit her on fire and terrified her at the same time. Her leggings hit the floor, meaning she was completely, utterly bare, while Chelsea still had her form-fitting dress on, fully clothed. All of those voices in her head threatened to rise, but Chelsea lifted her head instead, pressing her lips to Kyle's. The sweet contact silenced those voices at once.

Chelsea continued coaxing kisses out of her, and Kyle melted into them as they soothed the frayed edges of her nerves. Her bare ass rested on the couch cushions, and her pussy came close to gushing with how hot this woman made her. Chelsea trailed two fingertips down the middle of her chest, the touch leaving a searing line as she descended lower and lower. Kyle moaned into her mouth as those fingertips brushed against her folds.

"God, that's hot," Chelsea murmured against her mouth. She slid her fingers along her seam, continuing to nibble along Kyle's jawline, her earlobe, her neck. Staccato breaths escaped from Kyle as the headiness threatened to consume her. All she could feel was the inferno of warmth between them, and with every inhale, Chelsea's almond-and-leather scent caressed her.

Chelsea brushed her fingers over her clit, sending sparks through Kyle's entire system. She began to circle around the sensitized nub with the confident movements that turned her to jelly.

"Fuck, that feels amazing," Kyle gasped out, unable to help herself. Chelsea sank her teeth into the side of her neck, intensifying the sensations flooding through her. Her core ached, and she longed to have Chelsea driving her fingers inside her, claiming every inch of her, but the woman followed her own plan, teasing her to the point of explosion.

Chelsea continued with those tender bites along

her neck that were enough to make her delirious and drunk on the sensations. She dragged her fingers along Kyle's wetness before she continued to swirl against her clit, bringing her closer and closer. Each stroke caused new bliss to course through her veins, and the woman was relentless with the way she teased and coaxed the reactions out of her.

Kyle closed her eyes, surrendering to the way Chelsea crouched over her, how she possessed and claimed every inch of her with her teeth and tongue. Her fingers brushed against her clit over and over again to the point that her hips bucked up in response. She grew desperate for the release mounting inside her. Kyle gave over to the sensations controlling her, and Chelsea's mouth and fingers brought her to the edge.

The circles at her clit grew so intense her breath hitched and sweat beaded on the inside of her thighs. Yet Chelsea didn't pause for a moment, the firm pressure unrelenting. The initial throb heralded her impending release, and Kyle tipped her head back, a throaty moan escaping her.

Her clit thrummed, and Chels continued to touch her through her orgasm as the pulse spread from her clit outward, melting through her entire body. Flashes of light flared behind her closed lids like live sparks, and Kyle rode the waves of the intense orgasm, never wanting this bliss to end.

Slowly, she began to return to her body, feeling the couch cushions beneath her and Chelsea's weight on her thighs. She stared up at the woman before her.

Chelsea pulled back, just watching her, an expression of awe glazing her eyes. "I thought you'd look fucking gorgeous all blissed out like that, but I had no idea how much. You're a goddamn master-piece all splayed out beneath me."

Kyle flushed at the comment, but she'd become so relaxed the normal nerves didn't creep in with those compliments. "You're something else, Chelsea Moore."

Chelsea lifted her two fingers, wet with Kyle's slick, and sucked them into her mouth. The sight was so erotic that desire pumped through her anew, like she hadn't just experienced a fierce orgasm. Chelsea grinned. "I knew you'd taste sweet as sin."

"Now it's your turn," Kyle murmured, wanting to thrust her tongue between those thighs and devour this beautiful woman.

Chelsea shook her head, a smirk on her lips. "No, this was for you, sugar. Pop your clothes back on or don't, because I'm planning on unwinding with my neglected beer before we head to bed." Chelsea leaned in so her lips brushed against Kyle's ear. "If you're good, though, I'll let you lick my pussy tonight."

Lord, this woman would be the death of her.

CHAPTER TWELVE

CHELSEA KNEW GETTING TO STRIP KYLE DOWN would be intense, but hot damn. She'd never experienced the heady rush of connecting with anyone like this before. The way Kyle melted against her, how she let Chelsea pin her down and control the space between them offered more of a gift than the woman would ever realize. Noah had never surrendered to her that way, no matter how many times they'd fucked, which grew increasingly less and less over the years.

Kyle had reluctantly even listened when Chelsea switched from intense back to casual like whiplash. Not like she wasn't dying to experience everything the woman could offer. Her panties had been soaked from the moment this began, but she wanted Kyle to wait a little longer. She hadn't been lying when she said the woman's orgasm was for her alone. Kyle dealt with years of self-hatred heaped upon her to the point she couldn't take a single compliment without backlash.

No amount of babble would pierce through that. But Chelsea wanted her to feel possessed and treasured, every damn thing the woman deserved. Still, hanging back and watching *Buffy the Vampire Slayer* on Netflix ended up being pure torture—because she wanted more. She wanted Kyle splayed out on the bed and all the time in the world to explore those curvy hips, the taste of her juices, and those muscular legs.

Chelsea squirmed in her seat again, trying to ignore the slickness between her own folds at all the filthy thoughts rampaging through her mind. She'd worried she might feel a little unsure about her first time with a woman, but being around Kyle put her so much at ease that the new experience never mattered. She knew how to read the woman, and once they came together, each touch, stroke, and kiss felt so natural.

"Uncomfortable?" Kyle asked, her brow crooked and an amused grin on her face. She tipped back another sip of cider, the liquid glossing her pert lips.

Chelsea delivered her a look. "Enough of the sass. I regret nothing. Besides, we're watching Buffy right now."

"I'm watching," Kyle clarified, nudging her knee against Chelsea's. "You're either alternating between staring into space or giving me the sorts of hungry looks that are pure torture for both of us."

Chelsea sucked in her bottom lip. Kyle wasn't wrong. She hadn't been paying attention to the slaying shenanigans for a while now, not with Kyle curled against her and the heat from their bodies muddling her ability to think and to breathe.

"Damn you for making sense," she murmured. "Fine. Let's head to bed."

"Oh, thank fuck," Kyle exploded out, her open grin plucking a chord deep within Chelsea's chest. "This has been killing me."

Chelsea stood up from her spot on the couch and offered a hand to Kyle. Instead of accepting her hand, Kyle bent down and scooped her up into her arms, bridal style. The woman possessed the sort of muscles and sturdy frame to lift her with ease, and Chelsea's mind dizzied at the way Kyle had literally swept her off her feet.

"Come on, let's get you to the bed," Kyle

responded, carrying her across the room in strong strides. "Buffy can wait."

Chelsea wanted to melt against her. Normally this sort of comfort took years and years for her to build—hell, she couldn't say she'd ever trusted Noah as much.

Kyle nudged the bedroom door with her foot and carried her inside. She'd spent plenty of time in Kyle's bedroom already, but not with this adrenaline rolling through her. They'd dipped their toes in the pool together earlier, but this time, she'd be making the full plunge.

Kyle lowered her onto the bed with a gentleness that made her heart quicken. The woman stood before her, a slight grin quirking her lips. "I believe promises were made?"

"They were," Chelsea responded, slowly opening her legs wider. Kyle's gaze zeroed in on the movement. "With one stipulation. I want you to strip down."

Kyle had been so quick to yank her clothes back on, but if Chelsea got her way, this woman would be naked as often as possible. Her gorgeous body emanated strength, from those sexy thick thighs to her tapered waist. Her breasts fit her frame perfectly, with light nipples that were pure temptation to bite and tease. Every freckle up and down her body formed another mark on a beautiful canvas of creamy skin leading up to a gorgeous, earnest face.

"If it means I get to taste you, I'll do just about anything," Kyle murmured, sliding her tank top over her head.

Chelsea was dizzy with lust, drunk on it from tasting every inch of this woman earlier. The bites she'd left on Kyle's shoulders remained dark enough to linger, and she didn't realize how much marking Kyle would turn her on. The woman was a natural submissive, and they clicked in a way she never had before with another soul.

As Kyle brought her sweatpants and underwear down, leaving her bare again, Chelsea sucked in a sharp breath. God, she was hot. From the creaminess of her skin to the damp curls over her folds, Chelsea fought the temptation to just drag Kyle onto the bed and tease her until those moans exploded out of her again.

Chelsea offered a small nod and tugged her own dress up and over, tossing the fabric to the floor. She still wore her lacy black bra and panties, but she didn't bother taking them off. Her skin prickled slightly at the step into this new territory. She scooted back on the bed, and Kyle crawled toward her, the mattress shifting with her movements. Chelsea's legs trembled in anticipation of how badly she wanted this.

"Take my panties off," Chelsea instructed, loving how Kyle's eyes lit up at every order. Damn, the woman responded so beautifully. She wanted to play with her even more, but right now her core throbbed to the point she could scream, her clit tender and swollen. Kyle moved with a subtle grace, sliding her panties off in a quick motion. Her tongue dipped out to wet her lower lip.

"Bra too," Chelsea murmured. She wanted every piece of fabric between them gone.

Kyle leaned over her, a sweet brown-sugar-and-cinnamon scent drifting her way. Chelsea's mouth watered. She wanted to sink her teeth into the woman again and bite. She bet the insides of her thighs would taste delicious. Kyle unsnapped Chelsea's bra and dragged it off before tossing it over the side of the bed.

Her nipples pebbled, and the way Kyle's hot gaze raked over her whole body gave her a heady, intoxicating feeling. "Go ahead," Chelsea encouraged. "Explore all you like, sweetheart."

Kyle didn't need any more prompting. The woman's sensual mouth was on her skin the moment the words left her lips. Kyle hovered over her, dipping down to press kisses along her collarbone and between her breasts. The tender sweep of her lips sent butterflies swarming through Chelsea— everything this woman did was milk-chocolate sweet. Kyle brushed her thumb across Chelsea's nipple, and lust jolted through her in response. She needed Kyle's mouth on her now.

When she looked down, Kyle's gaze met hers, that care emanating through. The realization hit Chelsea—Kyle knew she'd never been with a woman before.

She reached to brush her fingertips along the side of Kyle's face. "Sugar, I'm not scared. I want this with you. I also might incinerate if I don't get your hot mouth on me soon, because it's been a long, long while since I had any action."

Kyle shook her head, though a grin lit her lips. "Bossy. Can't even let me enjoy this for let's say... a half hour or so."

Chelsea snorted. "Have you met me? Besides, you like it."

Kyle nodded, one of those beautiful blushes staining her cheeks like she'd been plucked out of a painting. Chelsea's heart thudded harder. God, this woman. She usually dove into sex rough and ready, a loud, willing participant, but everything between her and Kyle contained a different layer in the mix. The emotions that emerged to the surface were a rarity, but somehow extricating the two became impossible with Kyle Walker.

Kyle skimmed her hands down Chelsea's waist and her hips, and her whole body quaked in anticipation. She was so damn soaked at this point, yet every brush of Kyle's lips over her skin on the way down made her delirious. The woman looked fucking stunning as she settled between her legs, her shaggy auburn hair the perfect length to tug. Kyle's mouth pressed on the inside of her thigh, and Chelsea let out a low curse.

She sucked in a shaky breath, desperate for Kyle to place that hot mouth on her clit, inside her, anywhere. At this point, she'd take whatever the woman would give her. Kyle slipped her arms underneath her thighs and wrapped her hands around Chelsea's hips as she lowered her mouth to her folds. Her hot breath puffed against the sensitized flesh of her clit, and Chelsea let out a soft moan.

"Fuck, you're so damn pretty," Kyle murmured. Before Chelsea could even think of responding, those lips pressed to her pussy, and Kyle's tongue slipped out. The first lap against her clit hit like pure ecstasy. Chelsea's fingers dug into the sheets as Kyle began with slow, excruciating licks that sent sparks throughout her entire body. The woman was patience personified, a steadiness emanating from every movement as she licked and sucked at her cunt.

She blinked back stars with every firm stroke, and Kyle became unstoppable. Every time Chelsea caught her breath again, the woman would continue, her talented mouth coaxing moans from her with ease. She leaned up for a moment to catch a glimpse of Kyle between her legs, the sight of those swollen lips covered in her juices so damn hot. Kyle's intense hazel eyes skimmed over the length of her body. This moment was heady, perfect, and more than she'd ever imagined.

Kyle's steady strokes began to overwhelm her, each one given with enough pressure to make Chelsea's thighs quake a little more. Sweat beaded on her forehead, and she tilted her head back, surrendering to the thrill. The sheets were cool against her back, and the way Kyle's mouth brought her closer and closer made her toes curl. She'd faced some talented tongues before, but with Kyle there was this dizzying intimacy that threatened to overwhelm her as much as the intensifying sensations.

Kyle sucked her clit before she switched to thrusting her tongue inside of Chelsea, which pushed her right over the edge. Her nails dug into the mattress as her hips lifted. Her clit pulsed in waves violent enough that her legs shook. Kyle continued to lap at her clit through the orgasm as the bliss rolled through her like a brand-new day.

The intensity began to ebb as Chelsea lowered her hips to the mattress. Once she regained her senses, she crooked her finger. "C'mere."

Kyle crawled over top of her to plant a kiss on her lips. Chelsea sank into it, reaching up to grab Kyle by the waist. She loved the slope of those gorgeous hips. Their breasts crushed together when their kiss deepened, slow and languid as tongues dipped in and glided. Chelsea slipped her hand between them to drag her fingertips along Kyle's pussy. She was dripping. Damn if that just didn't turn her on all over again.

Chelsea continued to kiss her as she slipped two fingers in past the folds. Kyle let out a breathy moan, right against her mouth, and Chelsea began to pump her fingers inside the woman. She wasn't sure if she got this right, being her first time and all, but she'd masturbated an extraordinary amount and figured a similar technique couldn't hurt to try. Based on the way Kyle bucked her hips forward in response, she hadn't horribly fucked up, so she continued to pump her fingers in, finding her rhythm.

Kyle kissed along the length of Chelsea's neck, soft, desperate kisses that grew so hot they seared her mind. Their bodies crushed together, smooth and velvet skin mixed with sweat, and Chelsea drowned in the luxurious feel, everything enhanced in the wake of her orgasm. Kyle's breaths were gentle pants against her fevered skin as her eyes grew glossy. Chelsea wrapped her free hand around Kyle's waist, bracing the woman whose knees dug into the mattress a little more with every pump. Her hips lifted higher, that stunning ass on clear display.

Kyle's breath hitched as Chelsea quickened her pace, her thumb brushing against her sensitive clit.

"Come for me, beautiful," Chelsea murmured in her ear.

Within seconds, Kyle's pussy throbbed around her fingers with an orgasm, and she let out this beautiful moan that echoed in the night-darkened air of the bedroom. Chelsea continued to stroke her fingers inside until Kyle sank against her, sweat beading along her skin. Chelsea dipped down to lick along the nape of her neck, enjoying the salty taste. Slowly, she extricated her fingers, bringing her hands to rest around Kyle's hips.

She stared at the ceiling for a moment. The only sounds circulating through the room were their desperate breaths. She'd crossed the Rubicon for sure this time. A kiss she might be able to backtrack from, but not the mind-blowing sex they had tonight.

Clearly, she wasn't as straight as she'd thought.

And goddamn, if she believed one round with this woman would sate her curiosity, she'd been wrong, wrong, wrong. She wanted weeks, months, years to explore this.

"You're being quiet," Kyle murmured. "Are you okay?"

Chelsea glanced to meet Kyle's soft hazel gaze, slight concern crinkling her brow.

"You're my first, that's all," Chelsea responded, squeezing the woman by the hips in reassurance. "My brain's taking a moment to readjust."

"You don't fuck like someone who's never been with a woman before," Kyle muttered, extricating herself as she rolled onto her back right beside her. "Lord have mercy." She placed her arm over her forehead, allowing a beautiful glimpse of those gorgeous tits, pointed nipples, and the hips Chelsea had become obsessed with, all limned in moonlight.

Chelsea reached down to intertwine her fingers with Kyle's. "I don't regret a single moment. In case you were worrying."

Kyle's nose crinkled. "Am I that obvious?"

"Painfully so," she responded, an amused grin curling her lips. "But that's one of the things I enjoy about you."

"You're not uncomfortable about sleeping together afterward, are you?" Kyle asked. "I'm fucking exhausted, and I'm not relishing the prospect of lugging myself to the couch tonight. Though I will if that's where you're at right now."

Chelsea lifted a brow. "What gave you the indication I planned on doing anything but starfishing all over you tonight? Hope you don't mind fighting for the sheets, because I'm a nightmare to share a bed with."

"Good to know. I'll give you the forewarning that I'm a furnace," Kyle responded, reaching over to brush her thumb across Chelsea's lower lip. Chelsea's heart lurched at the tender motion. Raw affection bled from the woman's eyes. Even after what Kyle said about being tired, a moment later she pushed up from the bed and came padding back with washcloths for them to wipe up. They discarded them over the side of the bed, and Kyle turned onto her side, facing her. Her breathing began to even, and her eyes closed tight in slumber.

Chelsea curled on her side, watching the rise and fall of Kyle's chest, the sheets loosely covering her. She reached out and rested her hand on Kyle's waist, needing the anchor of touch right now. Her body might be exhausted and sated, but her mind raced.

The moonlight cast careless beams across the woman's cluttered dresser, her rumpled sheets, and the few framed prints lining the walls. Kyle's auburn hair took on a purple sheen, and her long lashes grew starker in the shadows. Those lips were slightly parted, full and lush after the way they'd clashed with Chelsea's tonight.

Chelsea swallowed hard.

She dove into this headfirst from the start. Fake girlfriend? Sounded like a blast. Curious about some power exchange? Fucking fun as hell.

However, as she lay here in bed with Kyle, she drowned in her presence, a mixture of sweetness and stability Chelsea had craved for so long. Yet how did she even begin to cross the chasm? All of the problems she'd run away from at Thanksgiving dinner threatened to rush to the surface, no matter how much she tried to stave them off.

She wouldn't be getting a wink of sleep tonight.

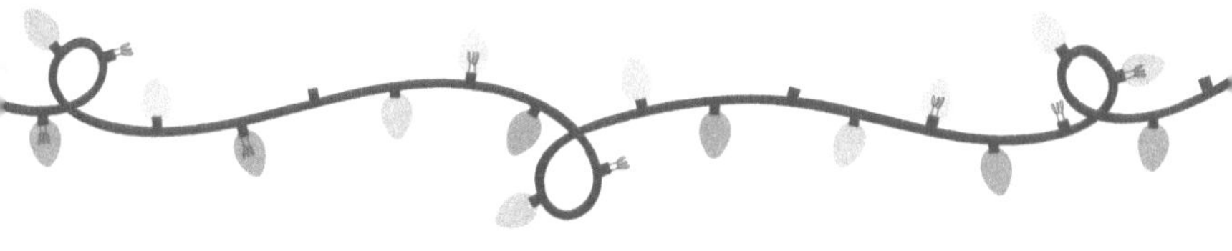

CHAPTER THIRTEEN

KYLE ADJUSTED HER GRIP ON THE MASSIVE TOTE of chocolate cherry cupcakes she carried up the brick pathway to Aubrey and Selina's. She and Chelsea had spent most of the day fucking in bed until she could barely feel her feet anymore. Each step reminded her of the delicious soreness between her legs from the way Chelsea had ravaged her. The woman was insatiable, demanding, and intoxicating.

No one had ever made her feel so possessed. The way Chels dominated her in bed somehow erased the usual jitters that normally came along with sex. She got so lost in sensation that she didn't worry like usual about her partner judging her bigger hips or hating her figure. When she was with Chelsea, she could just surrender to the pleasure.

Kyle didn't bother knocking as she grabbed for the knob, balancing the cupcake tray in one hand. Based on the car in the driveway, Chelsea had probably already arrived. They'd agreed to go separately so as to avoid spelling out their situation on a flashing Vegas sign. After all, her best friend had no idea Kyle was fucking her little sister, and she preferred to keep her out of this.

Considering she didn't even know what to even call the situation between her and Chelsea, she couldn't go announcing anything to her nearest and dearest. Fuck buddies? Friends with benefits? Every time she caught Chelsea's intense, possessive stare, it felt like more than that, but hell, Chelsea wasn't even out of the closet, and barely divorced at that.

She stepped inside, and the blast of warmth and murmured voices rolled over her. Even though a few jitters trailed at her heels, she sank into the comfort of their yearly tradition—the Thanksgiving dinner she actually looked forward to. Kyle strolled in, heading past the empty foyer filled with Wiccan symbols and dried herbs over the entryway and into the dining room where the voices were coming from. Selina and Aubs had decorated in full, a nice rich russet tablecloth over the table, small wire pumpkins scattered around, and all of the glossy plates already out.

The steaming casseroles and turkey sat on display in the middle of the table. When she walked in, Selina, Aubs, and Chelsea glanced up at her in unison. Chels's eyes softened, and her grin took on a wicked curve that traveled right to Kyle's core. Right. Hiding this would be a thousand times harder than she thought.

"Am I the last one here?" Kyle asked, continuing to walk toward the kitchen. "And where do you want dessert?"

Aubs shook her head and hopped up from the seat. "Sky and Mia are set to show any minute. You can put those delicious cupcakes right in my mouth. Or, I guess alongside the majestic pecan pie we bought from the store."

"Sky's bringing some fancy French shit she learned to make at Lumiere," Selina called over. "So we're waiting on that to get started."

"Oh, hell yeah," Kyle responded, following Aubrey as she led the way to the kitchen. "You know I'm here for Sky's cooking any day of the week."

"Don't forget the green-bean casserole I made," Chelsea called out. "You better give it a try."

Kyle tried to hide her smirk. Chelsea had

whipped the casserole together in Kyle's kitchen, and the woman had drawn her over for a taste which ended in a kiss. From there, the situation just got hot and heavy. A steady flush crawled through her body at the memories she fought hard to dispel as she stepped into Aubrey's kitchen where the pecan pie sat on the counter.

"I made enough cupcakes for an army, so they should cover dessert," Kyle said, placing the tray on the counter.

Aubs gave her a second glance over, nudging her in the side with her hip. "Did you get laid or something?"

"What?" Kyle's eyes widened, and the question burst out in a splutter.

"Fucking knew it," Aubrey said, her grin deepening and her eyes twinkling. "You seem way more relaxed than normal. There's a freshly fucked glow about you. Did you pick up someone at one of the bars around Thanksgiving? I know that's prime time."

Kyle shot her a look. "I'm not you, babe."

"But you definitely got laid," Aubrey said, amusement in her tone. "I noticed you're not denying that tidbit."

"Let's get to dinner and ignore my sex life," Kyle responded, flicking her in the arm.

Aubrey let out a low whistle. "Hell no. I'm going to pry the answer out of you some way tonight."

Kyle's stomach sank. At least Chels was a far better liar than she'd ever be. Kyle could keep avoiding direct answers, and Chels could continue on with her poker face so Aubrey wouldn't have to know.

She hoped.

The front door creaked open, and Kyle seized upon the interruption. "Looks like Sky and Mia have arrived." She sped out of the kitchen, even though Aubrey's stare burned hot on her heels. *Don't look at Chelsea. Don't look at Chelsea.*

Sky stalked into the dining room with a massive tray in her hands. "Hope you guys like cassoulet."

"I brought wine," Mia chimed in after. "Trust me, you don't want what I'd create in the kitchen."

Kyle strode up to them and gave Mia a quick hug before following Sky to offer her one too. Crap, she hadn't doled out hugs to everyone else. She turned around to see Aubrey standing behind her, giving a smug look with her arms open. Kyle grinned back, squeezing her best friend tight. She popped over to Selina and offered her a hug. Which only left

Chelsea. She could do this and not make things awkward or obvious. *Think about the inevitable heat death of the universe. Or dolphins. Or why the hell candy cigarettes were ever a thing.*

Kyle leaned down and gave Chelsea a light hug, even though she wanted to bury her face in the silken skin of her neck and taste her lips. The delicious scent of almond wafted off her, mixing with sex and sweat from earlier, even after the shower they took in the morning. Fuck, she wanted to just melt into her lap and stay there.

When Kyle forced herself to pull back, she happened to notice Sky and Mia had claimed the two seats on the opposite end, which left one open. Next to Chelsea, of course.

"Hon, do you want to say some sort of blessing to your pagan gods, or can we eat?" Aubs asked, elbowing Selina in the side.

Selina's lips curled in a feline smile, and she reached out to grab Aubrey and Mia's hands. "Everyone hold hands, since my darling girlfriend wants me to impose my religion on this gathering."

"Ugh, we get enough religion at my parents' place," Aubs muttered. "It was a joke." Even still, she reached out and grabbed Selina's and her sister's hands.

Kyle stretched out for Sky's hand first and then took Chelsea's palm in her own, trying to ignore how sparks trickled up her arm at the contact.

"Gaia, thank you for the bounty we share today." Selina squeezed hands with Mia and Aubs until the movement rippled around the table like a chain. Selina cast Aubrey an arch look. "I'd say that was far shorter than your father's litany, don't you think?"

"Thank fuck," Chelsea murmured, reaching across the table to grab her casserole dish and drag it over.

Aubs's brows lifted. "Is that criticism of our dear father falling from your lips? Please, let me lap up every crumb."

Chelsea scooped some casserole onto her plate and scooped a second helping, glancing to Kyle. "Want some?" She plopped the hefty bit on Kyle's plate.

"Wouldn't miss it," Kyle said with a grin, trying to expunge the heat from her voice, which was a feat in and of itself. She caught Sky's stare on her again, a curiosity there Kyle didn't like. Kyle reached forward and dug a spoon into the cassoulet as she met Sky's gaze head on. "Now let's try some of your fancy French shit."

"You'll dig the dish, Ky," Sky responded with a

grin, the tension between them diffusing. "It might be fancy French food, but it's comfort food."

"Sounds like my style," Kyle said as she placed a hefty helping onto her plate. The aromas wafted her way, rich and buttery, and she couldn't wait to eat. She'd scarfed down scraps of sustenance during the day, but between all of the time spent with Chelsea from Thanksgiving over Black Friday and into today, she'd barely eaten a full meal, and she'd fucked away any of those calories. Her pussy throbbed at the thought.

"Who had to dodge awkward conversations at Thanksgiving?" Mia asked, raising her hand. "My mom took it as a personal affront that I didn't fly out to Texas to see her, because how dare I have plans with my fiancée."

"Dad was a miserable dick at Thanksgiving again," Aubrey said, tearing into her buttered roll. "As per the norm. Though this time he dragged Chels into the mix too."

"Bully for me," Chelsea grumbled as she speared her casserole angrily.

Kyle chose that moment to shovel a forkful of Chelsea's green-bean casserole into her mouth. She sucked on the tines, enjoying the splash of flavors as

Chelsea's gaze drifted to hers, a small smile lifting her lips.

"What about you, Ky?" Aubs asked. "Was your mom a beast like usual?"

Kyle swallowed hard, the appetite leaving her at the mention of the woman. Honestly, the moment her brother moved out for good, she might not even visit for holidays.

"Excuse me, but I haven't finished complaining about Dad yet," Chelsea interrupted. Under the table, her knee knocked against Kyle's.

Fuck, she could kiss the woman for the save.

Aubs locked onto the critique of their father like a shark scenting blood. "Trust me, sis, I was pissed for you. Noah was the king of douchebags, and good riddance. Dad had no right trying to drag him into the fold again just because he missed having his buddy around."

"Ugh, that sucks," Mia chimed in, steering the conversation away from Kyle's mom and her constant criticism. Even still, Kyle fought to keep eating the food on her plate, unable to quite ignore the voice in the back of her mind that she'd gained too much weight and she shouldn't be downing as many calories. Mom's comments had killed one Thanksgiving dinner for her, and she wouldn't let her mother ruin this one. Still, she tried to ignore the phantom pinch of the measuring tape Mom had used time and time again growing up, dissatisfied with the way Kyle fit into her clothes.

Kyle reached out and grabbed another helping of mashed potatoes. Chelsea caught her gaze in the process and offered an approving nod, as if she knew what raced through her mind. She'd been falling fast for this woman, but now she careened.

After the initial prickle, the dinner passed fast with casual conversation and laughs as they railed on each other for random things, like the ridiculous way Mia ate her mashed potatoes, fluffing them into a tower she took bite after bite of, to Aubrey and Chelsea's sister wars of keeping the items on their plates separate or mushed together. She found it all too easy to imagine this future with Chelsea where they could all be here at the table cracking jokes.

One where she'd be going home with this gorgeous woman rather than returning to separate beds and separate lives.

Those thoughts were dangerous ones that had no grounding in reality. Chelsea was curious and interested, but they hadn't spoken once about whether or not she wanted anything serious, or even if she'd be willing to come out of the closet over this. The whole endeavor, from the fake-girlfriend beginning, created a recipe for heartache.

And yet, Kyle couldn't help but bake her own destruction.

After everyone had eaten, cleared their plates, and sat back enjoying feeling completely stuffed, Kyle caught Sky eyeing the kitchen a few times.

"Want me to bring out dessert?" she asked, an amused grin lifting her lips.

"I can smell the chocolate from here," Sky said, tilting her head toward the kitchen.

Kyle let out a laugh and pushed up. "I'll grab the cupcakes."

"I can get the pie," Chelsea volunteered. Kyle's heart thudded a little harder at the idea of being out of view for even a moment from the rest of her friends. They'd spent well over twenty-four hours with each other, but all that time wasn't enough. The incessant need to be around this woman had grown a thousand times worse than her sugar addiction.

Kyle hustled to the kitchen first, reaching for the small plates in the cabinet. She'd been in Aubs's kitchen enough to know this place backwards and frontwards.

Chelsea stepped in behind her, and once she ducked around the corner, the air between them tensed. Chelsea stared at her with those magnetic eyes, a wolfish, hungry look on her face that had nothing to do with the dessert. She took one step toward her, then another. Kyle backed against the counter, placing the dessert plates on the surface with a clink. Chelsea crowded into her space until their knees bumped together.

"Hey, you okay?" she asked, her voice no more than a whisper, the words puffing against her lips.

Kyle bobbed her head in a nod. "I finished my plate, didn't I?"

"Yeah, you did," Chelsea murmured, sliding her finger underneath Kyle's chin to lift it until their eyes met. "Good girl."

Fuck, those words undid her. If she hadn't already been turned on as hell, she might well have melted into a puddle here on the kitchen floor. Chelsea leaned in, brushing her lips against Kyle's in a tender kiss that clouded out any worry in the world. Whenever she spent time with this woman, somehow Chelsea quieted everything—the nerves, the awkwardness, the anxiousness. Kyle sank into their kiss, sweeter than any of the desserts they were about to bring out.

"What's taking so long?" Aubrey's voice erupted

—far too close. Ice jolted through her veins like she'd plunged into the Schuylkill.

She and Chelsea pulled back—too late.

By the time she stepped away, Aubrey stood in the entrance of the kitchen. Her eyes widened, and her jaw dropped. Oh, fuck. Chelsea gripped Kyle's arm tight, as if the motion might bolster her.

"What... the fuck is going on here?" Aubrey asked. Her words came out quiet, but Kyle knew better than to mistake them for anything but loaded with rage. The woman's eyes flashed as she glanced between them. Kyle swallowed hard. Not like she even had any answers to offer to Aubrey.

A realization crystallized in Aubrey's eyes as she swung her gaze like a scythe in Kyle's direction. "So, the person you slept with was my little sister?" Betrayal wrapped around her voice like thread to a spindle, tighter and tighter. "Are you goddamn kidding me?"

"Oh, fuck right off," Chelsea stepped between them, fire in her eyes. "You don't get a say in who I sleep with, Aubs."

"I fucking do if it's my goddamn best friend," Aubrey said, her voice rising.

Kyle speared fingers through her hair, not wanting to be here for any of this. She'd screwed up.

She'd massively screwed up, and now Aubs hated her. Aubs hated her, and she didn't even know what the situation between her and Chelsea meant. Her arms began to shake, and familiar heat pricked at her eyes. She was two seconds away from bursting into tears, but she couldn't do that here.

Seconds ago, things had been fine. But that look from Aubrey—*that look*.

Aubs would never forgive her.

"I've got to go," Kyle said, whipping around and striding away from the kitchen. Aubrey stepped forward as if she might try and stop her but then Chelsea stood in the way.

"No way, sis. This is between you and me," she said.

Kyle ducked her head and tried to ignore the stares from Selina, Sky, and Mia as she shuffled out. "I'll... just come and get my cupcake tray another time," she muttered. "I'm sorry." She cast one glance to the kitchen, knowing she was running away, but she couldn't handle this right now.

Maybe if Chelsea wanted her for real. Maybe if she hadn't already been feeling so damn lonely, like her friends were disappearing from her life. Kyle slung her jacket on in a numbing haze as she stepped out the door. The brisk air slapped her in the face, which didn't do much to stop the trembles running up and down her body.

She somehow reached her car, but it wasn't until she sat in the driver's seat and the door slammed that the floodgates burst open. Tears raced down her cheeks in a deluge, and her shoulders shook with her sobs.

Fuck, fuck, fuck.

Everything had become so messed up. Friendsgiving was her one safe haven from the world, and she'd gone and ruined it. She had no one to blame but herself. Kyle clutched the steering wheel like she might take the thing off, but she couldn't stop the sobs from flowing out. She should drive away, she should text Chelsea, she should go back in and try to explain herself... but none of those options felt remotely possible with the way her throat spasmed and how her eyes burned with those unchecked tears.

Kyle rested her forehead on the steering wheel, sagging against it as the tears continued to flow.

This was why she'd never have anyone. Because she ruined every damn thing she touched.

<h1 style="text-align:center">CHAPTER FOURTEEN</h1>

S TRIKEOUT FOR T HANKSGIVING NUMBER ONE, and now Chelsea struck out on Thanksgiving number two.

She wanted to head over to Kyle's the moment the woman walked out the door, but when she'd texted her minutes after she got fed up with her sister and ditched, Kyle shot a message back about needing some time to process. Chelsea hated being alone right now with these heavy feelings that pinched her skin like Botox, but she could respect the woman's need for space.

Which is how she ended up at Vintner's, the wine bar blended with speakeasy that had been one of her longtime hangs with her old friends and even during her relationship with Noah. She needed a taste of the past right now, of the brief moments she'd deluded herself that everything was okay. Chelsea settled into the familiar hardwood booth, the scent of aged port and polished wood thick in the air. The hazy amber lights drifted over her, illuminating the cracks in the exposed brick walls.

Aubrey wanted to push for answers, which ended with Chelsea following Kyle's cue to leave.

She knew her sister. Aubrey was as loyal as they came in defending the people she loved, but she also had the tact of an uppercut. The woman would plow right through a situation she didn't belong in. She wanted answers when Chelsea and Kyle had never even spent time talking about their relationship with each other.

Kyle hadn't pushed, and Chelsea hadn't volunteered, which led them to this impasse she didn't know how to cross. And now Aubs had discovered she'd dabbled on the other side of the fence, but her sister had never been the person in the family she worried about finding that information out.

No matter how shitty her relationship with Noah was, the whole boyfriend-girlfriend thing had been easy. He fucked off and had plenty of time with his guy friends, and she'd soldiered through on her own as she had become distanced from her own friends over the years. But family dinners were easy, holidays were simple—she'd never needed to worry.

Part of her felt a little selfish. She'd already plunged her head into the fire once with this divorce, raising the judgment of her immediate and extended family.

She couldn't deal with another massive change on top of that.

Even still, she might not get the choice. She took a sip from her glass of shiraz, enjoying the sharpness tonight. The truth never arrived sweetly.

Chelsea wasn't afraid of being alone, but this... uncertainty shook her.

A shadow fell over her booth.

"Is this seat taken?" a deep, familiar voice sounded.

Chelsea looked up to see the exact last person she wanted joining her for a drink tonight. Noah Dorchester. Thank fuck she never got around to changing her last name.

The man didn't look too different, even though they'd called it quits a few months ago. His dark hair was slicked back with product, though his blue eyes appeared a little more tired, and he'd shaved, which was so different from the scruffy guy she'd once fallen for. The things she'd once found attractive about him came off sleazy now, like the veneer had chipped away more and more over the course of the marriage.

Chelsea lifted a brow. "Are you asking if anyone's sitting there, or if I want your company?"

Noah sat down, because of course the bastard did. Not like he'd ever listened to her when they were together. "Why'd you block my number, Chels?" he asked, a plaintive note in his voice that grated on her nerves. Tonight was not the night.

Chelsea cast a quick glance to her cell phone. She'd gotten a barrage of texts from Aubs she planned on ignoring, but nothing from Kyle. All she could think about was the devastation in those hazel eyes as Mount Aubrey exploded all over the best friend who'd only ever supported her. "I would've thought you could put two and two together when I sent you the divorce papers, but then again, smarts were never your forte."

Noah crossed his arms and sent her a glare. "This whole thing started as a big misunderstanding in the first place. I get it—I took a job away from your family, from your career, and didn't ask you, but that didn't give you a right to divorce me."

Chelsea took a sip from her wine, though the smooth liquid failed to settle her nerves. She was three seconds away from walking out because his presence did nothing but irritate her. "No, you did me a favor by deciding to move away, since you provided the perfect opportunity to get rid of your ass. If you think I only divorced you because you took the long-distance job, you're sorely mistaken."

Noah's brows drew together. "That's not what your dad said."

Oh, fuck no.

Right now, the only person in the family who hadn't made it onto her shit list was Mom. Dad had no right to be spoon-feeding Noah false hopes just because he wanted to see her married off to some white-toast guy he approved of.

"Look," Chelsea said through gritted teeth. "You need to stop contacting my father. He doesn't speak for me, and I communicated my message loud and clear when I asked for a divorce. We've only got a few months left before this split is official, and I'm not changing my mind."

Noah shook his head. "Stop being stubborn, Chels. We were great together. You don't come across what we had every day, and the more I've been settling into the new job, the more I realized I made a mistake in letting you go without a fight. I want you back, Chelsea."

Chelsea choked on the hysterical laugh that bubbled in her throat. As much as she'd been bemoaning the loss of an easy relationship like the one she had with Noah, the whole thing had been lonely as hell. She'd felt more fulfilled in these past few weeks she'd spent with Kyle than she had throughout the entirety of her marriage, and that meant something. She tilted her wine glass to her lips and drank the dregs.

"If you're looking for a clearer answer, then hear it from the source, Noah," Chelsea said, placing her empty wine glass on the table with a click. "No matter what my dad might imply, we're divorced, and I'm done. We both made the mistake of letting a bad relationship go on far too long because it was convenient." Chelsea snagged her purse and rose from her seat. "Have a good night, Noah, and kindly leave me alone."

Noah's jaw clenched. Asshole never liked being told what to do. "I'll be back around Christmas. Just give us some thought."

A shrapnel laugh exploded from her as she took the first steps away from the booth. Chelsea turned around to flip him the finger. "Fuck off, Noah. No one wants you to fight for them."

At that, she marched right on out the door of the bar, rage alone carrying her at this point.

EVEN THOUGH KYLE had opened up the lines of communication, due to their mismatched schedules during the week, Chelsea wasn't able to get over to Kyle's apartment until Thursday. She'd blown through batteries on her vibrator at the memory of their transformative sex last weekend, but even more than that, she just missed the other woman. Something about being around Kyle settled her nerves in a way little else did, like pulling into the driveway at the end of a long road trip.

Chelsea strolled to the door, hesitation tugging at her arm as she lifted her fist to knock. Kyle had been pretty closemouthed on the subject of Aubs, but Chelsea didn't question for a second that things were still a mess. She'd been dodging Aubrey's calls all week, mostly because her sister kept demanding answers she didn't have. Chelsea rapped her fist against the surface, forcing herself to take the step forward.

She hadn't come any closer to sorting through

the muddle in her mind, but she had the feeling she was in good company with Kyle.

The thump of steps sounded, and a moment later, the door creaked open.

Kyle had rings under her eyes and a wan look to her features that seemed nothing like her normal incandescent glow. Chelsea's heart twisted in her chest. She'd caused this by getting involved with the woman in the first place. She'd always been a little reckless, but now Kyle had gotten wrecked for her impulsive decisions.

Chelsea reached out before she could help herself, her thumb trailing along the side of Kyle's face. At the touch, Kyle's features softened, and Chelsea's remaining restraint snapped. She closed the distance between them and brought her lips to Kyle's in a searing kiss. She'd been savoring memories of the woman's mouth all week, but they were phantom sensations compared to the heat exploding between them and how Kyle's sugar-sweet scent wrapped around her like a caress.

Chelsea stepped closer, wrapping her palms around Kyle's waist as she brought their bodies flush together. She stroked her tongue along Kyle's, teasing a moan from the woman that vibrated between them. God, this had been all she needed. When she was wound up tighter than a filament all week, she'd longed to taste this woman, to touch her, to simply be around her.

Kyle pulled away first, to her surprise. "As much as I love giving the neighbors a show, we should head inside."

Chelsea's lips curved with a grin, which widened when Kyle reached back to offer her hand. Chelsea intertwined her fingers through Kyle's as they headed inside her apartment and up the steps. This was the first real gasp of relief she'd experienced all week, and she planned on enjoying every minute.

"Has Noah tried bugging you at all since the run-in last week?" Kyle asked, glancing back at her as they reached the top of the steps.

"Fucker's back in Chicago, which means far away from me," Chelsea responded, leading them over to Kyle's couch. "Only a few more months until we're officially split." She flopped down onto it first, and Kyle took a careful seat beside her. She hated this distance that had crept between them since the incident on Friendsgiving, and the temptation grew strong to reach over and tug Kyle onto her lap. If she could kiss away any of the stress creasing the woman's forehead, she gladly would.

"Do you think he'll try to bug you again?" Kyle

asked, her voice cautious, as if she didn't want to cross any boundaries. Unless she was jealous.

The idea sent a silent thrill through Chelsea, but she hadn't been able to get a good read on Kyle like she could before. Aubrey's disapproval just might've soured everything before these hesitant feelings had a chance to blossom.

Was this what she wanted? A relationship with Kyle?

The real question lurked beneath the surface every time.

Was this connection between them firm enough to risk the devastation guaranteed to descend in her family?

A beeper sounded from the other room. Kyle offered a soft grin. "Hold on. Let me get that." The woman hopped up, and Chelsea enjoyed the view as Kyle's voluptuous hips swayed on her way to the kitchen. Her teeth itched to sink deep into those hips, to grip those thighs and devour her until she begged for release.

After a little bit of shuffling and the clank of a dish settling on the counter, Kyle returned into the room with a tray of what appeared to be chocolate chip cookies. The scent alone had Chelsea's mouth watering, along with the fox of a woman bringing them over.

"What are the chances of you stripping down and letting me eat them off your naked body?"

"Pervert," Kyle responded, a genuine grin reaching her eyes at last. "Chances are zero since I don't relish burns from head to toe."

"Right, so scratch the fireplay," Chelsea responded, heat climbing up her body. Some screw had turned loose in her brain if a simple smile from the woman got her this giddy, but she was ready to rock on her heels, thrilled for the first time all week. Her sleep had been a twist and roll of mangling the sheets at best, and she'd been tempted more than once to beg Kyle to let her crash at her place so she could just commute to work from there.

You know, like girlfriends. Fuck, she needed to sort this out.

Which meant she would have to talk to her family, or at least Aubs. The idea of the confrontation made her shrivel up again, at least until Kyle sat close enough that their thighs touched.

"Brown butter chocolate chip cookies," Kyle said, shoving the plate in her direction. "I've been stress baking."

"No word from Aubs?" Chelsea chanced, unsure

if she wanted to crack open the awkward topic or not.

Kyle's lips formed a thin line, and she shook her head. "I've been getting radio silence."

Christ, she wished she got that from her sister. Instead, Aubs grew more and more obnoxious with every text Chelsea ignored. The urge to distract rose in her, and she grabbed a cookie off the plate, enjoying the rich caramelized scent of brown butter and the piping hot chocolate, still liquid on the cookies.

She took a bite and let out a slutty moan. "Fuck, those are next level."

Kyle picked one up and nibbled on the edge. Her phone buzzed, and she grabbed it a little too fast. Her expression fell. "Just my aunt."

Clearly, she'd been hoping Aubrey would extend an olive branch or even a "fuck you" via text. Not her stubborn sister.

Kyle sucked in a deep breath. "She was asking again if you're coming to the Christmas party in two weeks."

"Oh, shit," Chelsea said. "I'd almost forgotten about the fake-girlfriend gig."

The moment the words left her lips, she knew they were the wrong ones. She knew the real ones she wanted to say, but they crumbled on her lips every time she tried to voice them out loud. With her family in shambles around her and ex-husband harassing her, her life had become too much of a wreck for more complications.

Trouble was, Kyle felt like anything but a complication. Somehow, amidst all of this, she'd become a safe place.

Kyle's gaze dropped, and Chelsea sucked in a sharp breath. She reached out to grab Kyle's hands. "Hey, I'll be there. I wouldn't miss your family shindig for anything."

"Appreciate it," Kyle murmured, even though she wouldn't look up at her. "All the stressing over being able to sell the façade seems silly now that we've slept together."

"What's with the past tense?" Chelsea asked, reaching over to tip Kyle's chin up. She needed to look into Kyle's deep-set eyes—needed to know everything was okay. "I'm going to keep fucking you until you get sick of me." Even with her playful tone, vulnerability prickled up her spine. She wanted to make broad declarations, but she was terrified of scaring Kyle away—and even more freaked out about what came with those declarations.

Maybe once things calmed down. Maybe then....

Kyle looked at her, those beautiful hazel orbs filled with a hummingbird hope that made her chest ache. "Please, like anyone could get sick of you."

Chelsea leaned in, closing the space between them. Her lips brushed against Kyle's, and she swept her tongue inside the woman's mouth. Goddamn, she tasted so good, the burst of chocolate, salt, and brown sugar from the cookies all in there. Kyle melted into the kiss, resting her palms around her waist. Chelsea sank into the luxurious feel of those plush lips, the heat of her mouth, and the slow, languid rhythm they found together.

She nudged Kyle's legs open as she climbed on top of her while beginning to push her back on the couch. All too fast she hovered over Kyle, palms digging into the couch on either side of her as she devoured her mouth.

They broke for air for a moment, breaths explosive between them. Chelsea's hair drifted past her shoulder, the strands tickling her skin. Kyle watched her with a dreamy expression on her face, one that made her want to claim, to possess.

"I think we've both had horrible weeks and deserve a little stress relief," Chelsea murmured, her lips a breath away from Kyle's.

"If it means more of that, I'm in," Kyle

responded, a little breathless as she stared up at her. Chelsea's heart thudded a little faster at the sight of the woman spread beneath her looking far too gorgeous for her own good.

"Happy to oblige," Chelsea responded, a streak of lust tearing through her.

Right here, she could shut out all of the outside stresses and forget what a wreck her life was.

Right here, she could lose herself in the taste of this woman, the feel of her.

Right here, she was safe.

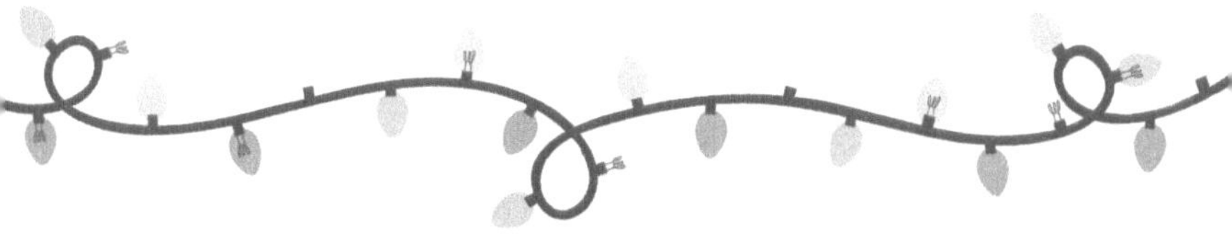

CHAPTER FIFTEEN

Kyle's heart thudded a little harder as she approached the red-bricked townhomes lining the street. She'd never been to Chelsea's place before, and as much as her curiosity had grown maddening, she didn't want to broach the subject. The woman guarded her secrets like she was Smaug in the Lonely Mountain, and Kyle could be patient. Slowly, Chelsea had begun to offer more and more of her worries, her past relationships, private things that she could've never learned from Aubs.

As her feet pounded along the walkway, she winced. Her best friend still hadn't said a word to her, despite the texts she sent. The lack of a response was unlike Aubrey, but fucking her sister was also unlike Kyle, so they had both waded into unfamiliar territory. Sky and Mia kept her sane right now. Both of them texted her through the week, trying to make plans to hang and reassuring her that their friendship hadn't changed at all. That she wasn't alone.

Still, her heart ached. If she lost Aubs, she didn't know what she'd do. They'd been best friends for such a long time, and she couldn't imagine a world without the woman in it. But she couldn't stop seeing Chelsea either.

Kyle reached the front door that was softly lit by the outside lantern. The night brought brisk breezes and the skitter of dry leaves and parched twigs along the pavement, but once Chelsea opened the door, all she could feel was warmth.

Chelsea wore slouchy yoga pants and a barely-there camisole with fabric so thin her nipples peaked the moment the brisk breeze slid her way. Her smile brightened, even though she glanced back into the house as if she were unsure about having visitors.

"Come on in," she said, brushing a light kiss to Kyle's lips before she started to follow. Even the brief contact sent a ripple down her spine. The woman had become chocolate-chip-cookie addictive.

"With the amount of secrecy you've shrouded this place in, I was pretty sure I was approaching a murder den," Kyle said as she soaked in the foyer, the main hallway, and the narrow staircase to the second floor. This place was all neat lines and bland landscapes on the wall, none of the surroundings capturing Chelsea's vibrancy. "Though," Kyle continued. "I guess you could be hiding the tarp-lined room in a secret closet or something."

Chelsea snorted as her fingertips skated along the rail of the staircase. "I wish I hid something as cool as a splatter room. I hate being here, that's all. This place reminds me way too much of how I let Noah take over my whole life. Most of this house is decorated to his tastes, not mine, and I got so wrapped up in trying to make him happy and trying to make things work that I never even understood how much of myself I'd lost."

Kyle closed the space between them, resting her hands on Chelsea's shoulders, which had tightened during the process. The woman kept her pain bound up tight, but she clearly still struggled with regrets from all the time she'd wasted with Noah. Kyle swallowed hard. As much as she longed for answers, and as much as she needed to know if Chelsea felt something for her in return, she couldn't bring herself to ask because of that.

As she began to knead at her traps, the woman let out a low moan.

"You keep doing that and I'm going to drag you upstairs and fuck the hell out of you," Chelsea murmured, the woman's dark, commanding gaze making her wet from one look alone.

Kyle's lips curled in amusement. "Thought that was the plan tonight, anyway."

"Yeah, but part of the plan had been behaving like a reasonable host and offering you a drink, or something at least, before I accosted you." Chelsea said, not budging as Kyle continued to work along the scalenes in her neck, her upper traps, and down her erector spinae on either side of the spine. Having her hands on that soft, hot skin was no hardship, and as she continued to work on her, she fought the urge to sink her body against Chelsea's.

"Fuck reasonable," Kyle murmured, her voice soft. "I've been thinking about you taking me all week."

With Chelsea, the sex was more intense than any she'd experienced, but her need for this woman grew ravine deep—far more than physical. When Kyle was around her, the insecurities faded away for a few brief moments. She'd felt awkward and gawky in her body for so long, like every time she stepped out into the world, shame coated her in a hard candy shell. Chelsea silenced those voices with the way she touched, the way she claimed, the way she possessed. The relief was monumental.

Chelsea pivoted to tug on the belt loops of Kyle's jeans, bringing their bodies flush together. "Look at you, sweetheart, talking all sexy-like. You're already so irresistible I'm tempted to strip you down here and eat you out on the steps."

Kyle shook her head, her grin widening at the filthy way Chelsea talked. She was like that with everything—frankly sexual and honest, even amid all of the things she kept shrouded. "There's one thing I want to see before we head to the bedroom."

Chelsea tilted her head to the side, even though she didn't let go of her belt loops, the secure hold making Kyle's mind reel.

"What's the room in this house that belongs to you?" Kyle asked, barely believing she had the audacity to ask. "The one that reminds you of Noah the least. I want to see that one." She might push with close friends, but around this woman she tended to lose all sense of coherency. And she'd rarely been with anyone long enough to feel comfortable like she did with Chelsea Moore.

Chelsea's gaze softened, and she glanced up the staircase. For a moment, Kyle thought she might refuse, that she'd back away from the request.

"Come on, follow me," Chelsea said, letting go of her belt loops to extend a hand. "I've managed to reclaim one room in the house because he barely used it to begin with."

Kyle placed her hand in Chelsea's as they ascended the staircase. The place smelled crisp like lemon cleaner and wood polish, but mostly unlived in. It felt so sterile and different from the way Chelsea sprawled around Kyle's apartment and filled in the empty corners like she'd always been there. Chelsea had even left her Nintendo Switch to charge recently because she'd be over soon enough anyway. If only this were something more. As much as Chelsea shared her affection and her desire, they'd never talked about commitment or a future beyond the here and now.

Women like her didn't tie themselves down to Kyle though. They might be good for a quick fuck or to sate some curiosity, but no one wanted her long-term. She couldn't hold onto hope for forever.

Chelsea squeezed Kyle's hand a little tighter, as if she could sense her mind roaming. The woman read her better than anyone else. They headed down the hallway and past a few closed doors to one on the opposite end.

"Here's my space," Chelsea murmured, letting go for a moment to turn the knob and step inside.

Kyle followed in after her. The scent of incense lingered in the room, a few unburnt sticks gathered in a holder on the desk in the far corner. Most of the place was cleared out, all polished hardwood floors and gauzy, brightly colored fabrics that draped from the ceiling, adding bright splashes of color. Plenty of space spread out in the center, and around the edges were neatly stacked arm weights, a few yoga mats, and mini speakers.

"My workout room, sans Noah's stupid treadmill that I took to the curb," Chelsea murmured, casting a glance to the empty spot to the right side of the room. "I used to do performance belly dance. It's something I want to get back into at some point, but who has the time? My agenda's loaded with getting divorced, tons of responsibilities on the marketing team for those stupid headphones, and all of the bullshit that comes with taking care of a rental house by yourself."

This. This was the room that spoke of Chelsea, all strong scents, sweat, and bright colors. Kyle couldn't help but savor the glimpse into the woman, knowing for a fact Chels didn't show this area to just anyone. As much as Chelsea could be blunt and honest at times, she kept her deeper secrets private, and every door opened between them was a deliberate decision.

She didn't think she'd ever fallen this hard before—every detail about the woman thrilled her, and the more she got to know Chelsea Moore, the more she careened.

"As someone who's always been alone, that's why I stuck with apartments," Kyle murmured, running fingers through her short strands. Not like she'd chosen it that way. She'd longed for the sort of relationships her friends were involved in, but every time she thought she found one, it crumbled.

She could easily dive into the excuses of no one finding her attractive, that they all got tired of her after a while, but how many had she disclosed the truth about her insecurities to? Chelsea whittled those away with her loyalty, her constant compliments, and how she always tuned in on Kyle's emotional state. When she glanced up, Chelsea's gaze gleamed hot on hers.

The woman crossed the space between them, and Chelsea's thumb skimmed her bottom lip. "I know this look. None of that."

Kyle stared into those eyes, mesmerized. This close, Chelsea's almond scent shrouded her in fragrant sensuality, and her dark waves cascaded down her shoulders, begging to be stroked. She summoned her courage. Even if Chelsea broke her heart into a thousand pieces, even if all of this was a passing curiosity for the woman, she wanted to be here with her.

"Thank you for showing me this."

Chelsea dipped her head in a nod. She took a moment to clear her throat before she reached for Kyle's hand, lacing their fingers together. "Come on, sugar. I made some promises I have every plan on fulfilling."

Chelsea led them down the hall with confident strides before pausing in front of the middle door. She pushed it open, and the scent of fresh linens and a cool wintry breeze filtered her way.

"Sorry, I had the window opened a crack. Do you need me to close it?"

The sight on the bed arrested Kyle, her whole body flushing from head to toe. Cream sheets had been spread out on the made bed and resting in the center was a strap-on and a pair of black leather restraints.

"You can leave the window open," Kyle murmured, unable to suppress the liquid heat rolling through her at the thoughts of what they'd get up to tonight. Chelsea hinted they'd be dabbling around with a bit more, but Lord have mercy, this woman was more inventive in bed than she could've ever imagined.

A wicked grin lit Chelsea's features as she made her way over to the bed. "Like what I've got in store for you tonight?" She strolled nearer to her until she came close enough to grab hold of Kyle's jacket and slide it off her shoulders. "Time for you to get nice and comfortable, sugar." Chelsea continued to circle her, those confident movements bubbling straight to her head like too much prosecco.

Next, Chelsea plucked the hem of her T-shirt and slipped it up and over. Kyle helped by shrugging out of it and tossing the fabric to the floor. At that point, she immediately went for the button of her jeans, snapping them open and bringing the zipper down with a snick. Kyle kicked her shoes and socks off, allowing the jeans to slide down her legs before she nudged them to the side as well. Chelsea's fingers skimmed her bare skin, the woman constantly teasing and touching, which fast made her delirious. Her nipples hardened in the air under Chelsea's intense gaze.

"God, do you know how hot it is that you're never in a bra?" Chelsea murmured, sliding in front of her and cupping her tits, brushing her fingers over the tips of her nipples. Wetness pooled between Kyle's legs, soaking her boy shorts. "Now, off with these," Chelsea said, hooking a finger in the waistband of her underwear before pulling it down. "And get on the bed to wait for me, sweetheart."

Kyle all but leapt onto the bed, her ass hitting the pristine sheets, which were cool under her skin. Not like the slight chill mattered with the way those sensual touches and words made her blaze inside. Chelsea climbed over her, still fully clothed. She grabbed the pair of restraints and brought Kyle's arms overhead before fixing the supple leather around them. She gave a couple of yanks at the chain between them, and Kyle's arms moved.

"Comfortable?" she asked. "I figured we could begin to dip our toes in."

Kyle was about to nod when she remembered the earlier times they'd played together. "Feels good."

"Perfect," Chelsea said with a wink. Her tone was throaty and husky, like whisky on the rocks. "Now lay on the bed like a good girl and wait."

Chelsea hopped off the bed and began to strip down nice and slow, drawing her camisole overhead, the pale fabric a perfect contrast to her tan skin. Her nipples were tight and perfect buds Kyle wanted to suck on, and the slope of her hips promised sin. She hadn't forgotten just how damn good the woman tasted. Chelsea peeled down her yoga pants next, putting her skimpy black thong in full view.

Kyle lay on the bed, cool sheets pressed to her back, her wet pussy on display with her arms pinned above her from the restraints. Her chest rose and fell with the ragged breaths that escaped while she watched the woman slide the straps of the harness up her smooth thighs, fixing it in place. Chelsea pushed the dildo in through the center opening next.

"You have no idea how long I've wanted to fuck you like this," Chelsea murmured, centering the dildo as she began to approach. "You look so damn beautiful."

Rarely did she feel that way, but bound up and placed on display under Chelsea's hungry gaze, Kyle shed her normal vulnerabilities.

Kyle's pussy pulsed at the sight in front of her. The idea of Chelsea ramming the length inside her, filling her up and controlling her orgasm had her mind spinning. Her thighs tightened with the temptation to draw her legs together, but she left them spread. The glaze of desire in Chelsea's eyes as she scanned her body was worth the vulnerability.

Chelsea joined her on the bed, her knees dropping onto the mattress in front of her. She crowded into the space between Kyle's legs, leaning down to sink her teeth on the inside of her thigh. Kyle's hips bucked up at the mix of pleasure and pain, the sting causing her clit to throb with need. Chelsea reached up to draw two fingers along her slit, trailing through her slick.

"What do you want, sugar?" Chelsea asked, rubbing her fingers along Kyle's clit.

Kyle licked her lips, and her gaze trailed toward the length on the harness. "I want you to take me, completely."

"Fuck, that's hot," Chelsea purred. She climbed over top of Kyle, strands of her silken hair brushing across her skin. "You look like a dream spread out on the sheets for me."

A steady flush rose through Kyle's body at the focus of the scorching gaze on her. Chelsea made her feel desired like no one had before, in a way that sent her tripping over herself to do anything to please her. Even exposing herself—because Chelsea always, always made the effort worthwhile.

Chelsea dipped down to press her lips against Kyle's, deepening the kiss with the caress of her tongue. Their breasts brushed together, the tips of Kyle's nipples grazing against that impossibly soft skin. Sparks raced through her body as Chelsea continued devouring her mouth like she'd been starving. Chelsea's length glided against her seam, and the breath hitched in Kyle's throat. A moment later, the head of the dildo brushed between her folds, this time controlled by Chelsea's firm hand.

The woman continued to kiss her with tongue and teeth as she guided the length into her, inch by inch. The thickness stretched at her walls, and Kyle's breaths came out staccato in response. Kyle let out a hearty moan at the intrusion, at the way the woman sank deeper and deeper inside her. Chelsea continued to push further until she slid in all the way. The heat of Chelsea's body over top of her, feeling her press inside like she owned her, and the undulating caress of her mouth tipped Kyle into delirium. Her senses were overloaded, and the connection between them burned stronger than ever.

Kyle looked up at her, the fullness sating an ache she'd needed filled. With her arms bound overhead, her chest exposed, and Chelsea fully seated inside her, she felt so claimed that her eyes burned from the intensity. Emotions she'd never expected during sex bubbled up, like her scabs had all been torn open and she bled. This sort of vulnerability with a partner was unlike anything she'd ever experienced, and she'd never find the likes of it again.

"Please" came from her lips, a strangled, desperate sound. She didn't know what she begged for, but once the words left her, Chelsea began to rock inside. The movements made her delirious as her walls squeezed around the length. Each time Chelsea rammed in to the hilt, the smack against Kyle's clit sent flares throughout her body, intensifying every sensation. The woman hovered over top of her, her palms digging into the sheets on either side and her corded arms flexing with the movements.

Chelsea started out slow with long, languid strokes, but all too quickly she surrendered to the same desperation that crawled through Kyle's veins. It was like they'd found this immense, immeasurable joy which could get stolen away in a single moment. Chelsea rammed into her harder, faster, the mattress creaking around them. All Kyle could smell was the sweat on their skin and the leather of the restraints pinning her in place, and all she could feel was the delicious sting every time Chelsea ground into her, sinking inside like they'd connected on a different plane of existence.

Kyle closed her eyes, letting the sensations carry

her away as her hips bucked a little more with each stroke and her moans grew more desperate. Close. She was so close. Chelsea's heaving breaths mingled with her own as they both bucked and thrashed in this intense dance, magnetically drawn together again and again and again. Skin smacked against skin, and Chelsea thrust in again, a little deeper this time. Kyle's pussy throbbed in response as she careened over the edge.

She tipped her head back, surrendering to the pulse of her orgasm as that bliss cleansed all thought from her mind. Kyle floated away on the high as her hips thrust up, her thighs stiffened, and her pussy continued to throb around the length driving inside her. Blinding white light sparked behind her eyelids as she got caught in that swirl of ecstasy. A moment later, Chelsea let out a guttural groan and sagged forward, sliding in all the way as she stilled. Chelsea's limbs quaked in response, a whole-body tremor that rocked through her.

For a moment, their harsh breaths continued to explode like fireworks, the one sound in this charged room. Kyle eventually settled into her body again, her sticky skin pressed against the cool sheets with Chelsea looming over top of her. She looked up at the woman, and the tenderness in her eyes struck her square in the chest. Exposed like this, she had no defenses against that look, one that both launched her into a stratosphere of new hope and twisted her insides in the same breath.

Chelsea dipped down and pressed a sweet kiss to her lips, their skin brushing together, their breasts crushed between them. Kyle's heart fluttered then and there, and she knew she was screwed.

She'd told herself the entire time that this was temporary. If Chelsea wanted more—if she wanted a real relationship out of this, she would've claimed it by now. Kyle had convinced herself to live in the present, to enjoy the woman's company while she had it. She'd believed, foolishly, that she'd be able to survive the wreckage of this with her heart intact, or at least, be able to pick up the shards in the aftermath.

However, the truth was, she'd well and truly fallen in love with Chelsea Moore.

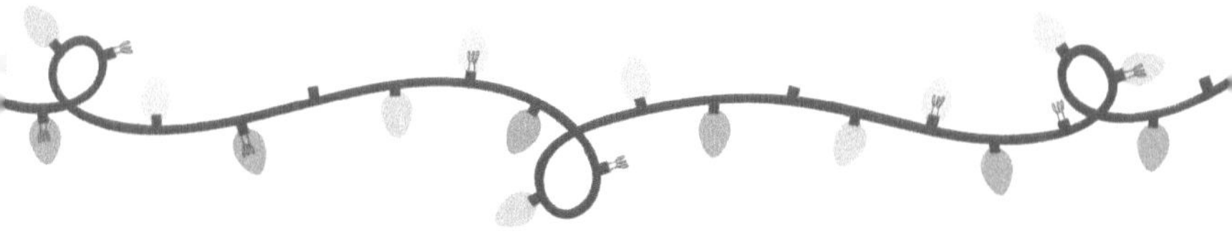

CHAPTER SIXTEEN

CHELSEA WOKE EARLIER THAN KYLE, AND AFTER spending a disturbing amount of time just watching the woman sleep, she pushed herself out of bed. Having someone in this bed felt familiar, but that person being Kyle meant so much more. When she and Noah got divorced and he moved out, everything they'd created here together mocked her. For the first time in a long while, the walls of this house didn't inch in more and more with an oppressiveness that made her feel claustrophobic.

Kyle was responsible for that—she knew this truth deep down.

Chelsea slipped on plaid pajama pants and a tank top before heading to the kitchen and beginning to work on pancakes. She had energy to spare and wanted to surprise Kyle when she woke up.

Her heart thudded a little harder at the memory of last night as she poured batter onto the sizzling pan. The connection between her and Kyle had been intense and electric from the start, but something had solidified and settled into place over the past few days. She'd been waiting for this feeling, like the ding of leveling up in a video game once she gained enough experience, the sign that indicated maybe, maybe it might be time to confess how she felt.

Chelsea flipped the pancake, enjoying the scent as the sides darkened to a chestnut brown. She wasn't blind. She could tell Kyle had been holding back from the start and letting her steer the ship. The woman had given her time and space when she'd needed it the most, and that couldn't have been easy with the sorts of insecurities Kyle struggled with.

A creaking sound came from the steps, and when Kyle turned the corner, Chelsea's heart took flight. The woman's short auburn hair was tousled, a few strands sticking up, and the sleepy look in her hazel eyes made Chelsea want to pin her against the wall. She just wore her tank top from yesterday and a pair of boy shorts, the sight exposing her long, muscular legs that Chelsea had all but developed a fetish for.

With the slight spray of freckles over her nose and those biteable, pink lips, Kyle Walker was one of the most beautiful women she'd ever seen.

"Damn, you're making pancakes?" Ky said, walking toward her. She stepped beside her and wrapped her arms around Chelsea's waist, resting her chin on her shoulder. Chelsea let out a low hum, trying to resist the urge to melt against her.

"Thought we'd both worked up enough of an appetite last night. Plus, a little birdie told me the way to your heart is through carbs," Chelsea murmured.

"Please, like you didn't have that from the start," Kyle responded, pulling her hands away for a moment to rub her eyes. She paused and glanced over at her, a bit of panic flaring in her gaze. If Chelsea had any sense, she should step in and say something, but she didn't want to just dump her feelings on Kyle like this at random. She wanted to sort these thoughts out and make her confession as clear as possible, something they could both look back on and remember.

"Uh," Kyle said, ruffling her hair before Chelsea could say anything. "You ready for the Christmas party next week?"

"I'll be there with bells on," Chelsea responded,

careful to not bring up the fake-girlfriend aspect. There was nothing fake about the way she felt toward Kyle. "I've got my dress picked out and everything."

"Don't get your hopes too high," Ky muttered, taking a seat at the breakfast nook. "It'll likely be a shit show, with my folks being either rude or cold. Dice roll as to which one. Mom still doesn't expect me to bring anyone, despite me telling her for the past month I will be."

Chelsea shook her head. "Hey, anything's better than the awkward Christmas I have to look forward to. Aubs is still pissed, and I don't know how to handle Dad."

"With the Noah stuff?" Kyle broached. "I know you and your dad are close, so it's got to be tough being at odds with him."

Chelsea flipped the last pancake off the skillet and brought the stacks over in two plates to where Kyle sat. She snagged forks and syrup before joining her on another stool. If only her issues were just the Noah stuff. Kyle's hazel eyes remained on her, concern clearly expressed by the crease between her brows. Chelsea might take her time to trust, but if anyone deserved that faith, Kyle did.

"No," she murmured, beginning to coat her

pancakes in syrup before passing the bottle over to Kyle. Her chest pinched tight, but she pushed through the discomfort anyway. "The Noah thing's the tip of the iceberg. I've been my dad's favorite for years because I dated guys and kept the peace. He and Aubs fought so much growing up that I was worried about the family fragmenting, and I ended up becoming the glue. Which is probably why I dealt with Noah's bullshit for as long as I did."

Her heart twisted tight at the truth hanging heavy in the air between them. She'd never admitted those words out loud before.

Kyle's gaze softened, and she reached out to squeeze Chelsea's thigh. "That must've been tough."

She didn't confide in anyone like this, but Kyle Walker was just different. She'd taken the time to coax Chelsea out rather than stampeding over her.

Chelsea shrugged, trying to ignore how her eyes heated. "Not only does Dad disapprove of my divorce with Noah, but once he finds out I'm not straight? Our relationship will implode. He'll ice me out, the same way he's done with Aubs all these years, and right now, she's too pissed to even be in my corner."

Kyle chewed on her lip. "I'm sorry." Guilt laced her tone, drawing Chelsea's gaze.

Chelsea shook her head. "You have nothing to be sorry for. You've been the one person keeping me sane through all of this, sugar." She closed the distance between them and placed a light kiss on Kyle's lips, hoping to reassure her. She savored her soft mouth and the sweetness that tingled through her at the gentle touch. When Chelsea pulled back, Kyle offered her a genuine smile, one that peeled back her layers every time.

"Okay, I've unloaded enough heavy shit on you first thing in the morning. These pancakes are going to get soggy, and we can't have that," she said, stabbing into the stack with her fork.

"Hence why I waited to douse mine," Kyle said with a smirk. She poured the syrup on her pancakes fresh. With the tines of her fork, Kyle broke into them and took a bite. "Goddamn, woman. You really can cook. These are delicious."

The blissed-out expression on Kyle's face had her heart thumping into overdrive. Something about this woman captivated her every time—each minute detail meant to be absorbed and savored like aged wine.

Chelsea took a bite, the sweetness of the maple syrup exploding on her tongue. She chewed, hoping the pancakes would stabilize the hollowness that opened in her belly at the thought of what she had yet to face.

First, she needed to tell Kyle how she felt.

Then, she had to smooth things over with her sister.

Last, she'd have to summon all of her remaining courage and finally face her father.

After a long day of massage clients, Kyle wanted to sink into her couch with takeout and Chelsea, both of which were on their way.

Her phone buzzed, so she grabbed it without looking and answered the call. "Kyle here."

"Dear, it's about time you responded."

A pit opened in Kyle's stomach at the sound of her mother's voice. The woman never failed to make her feel uncomfortable, a skill she'd honed to perfection from childhood on. "What's up, Mom? I meant to get back to you about the questions from earlier."

The passive-aggressive questions had hinted if she did have a girlfriend and brought her, that might place the aunts and uncles in an uncomfortable situation. Kyle hadn't wanted to touch those conversations with a hazmat suit and decontamination gloves, let alone respond. In fact, with every text her mother sent, the temptation to just snap and cut her out entirely grew stronger and stronger.

"You aren't actually bringing a girlfriend to the family party, are you?" Mom asked, the incredulous tone in her voice like a tuning fork trained on her sensitivities.

"Yeah, Mom, I am," Kyle ground out. Even as she said the words, though, the hollow ache in her chest bloomed anew. Truth be told, she'd be taking a fake girlfriend to parade around the family. Chelsea never made her any promises. After the other night, she'd never felt more vulnerable, yet she'd never been more confused as to where they stood. Chelsea wasn't even out yet, and Kyle would never force her to be.

Kyle swallowed hard.

"Do you think your... girlfriend is going to want to be uncomfortable too?" Mom continued, pushing. "You've got to make sure you don't let her slip away, Kyle. It's not like you have a lot of choices when it comes to dating."

Bile rose in Kyle's throat. Every time, Mom went for the jugular. Every time, the woman reminded her she wasn't worth fighting for, that no one would parade her around, let alone keep her. And as much as she wanted to fight back and argue her mother was wrong, life had proved that to be the truth.

Even Chelsea had never staked any claims. They were friends who fucked, and Kyle was the fool who'd gone and fallen in love.

"Look, you were the one who pushed in the first place. I'll be there with my date, and everyone can just deal," Kyle responded between gritted teeth. Even still, she couldn't help the lacerations that opened right up at Mom's comments.

"I'm saying you don't have to bring anyone if you don't want to," Mom responded. "No one's going to think less of you if you leave the girlfriend at home."

Of course, after all the jabs and comments, now that she made the commitment to bring someone, Mom had gotten cold feet. The truth was, Mom never expected her to show up with a girlfriend. The woman didn't believe anyone would find her worthwhile enough to fight for, to stay around for, to face awkward family functions for.

"What, scared I'll bring someone?" The words rose in her throat unbidden. "That I'll offer proof of the fact I'm gay, which means you can't keep denying it?"

"Kyle, you can't blame me for being disbelieving

when you've never brought anyone home," Mom cajoled in a condescending tone that always struck her match.

She couldn't take those barbs anymore.

"I can," she responded, her eyes beginning to sting with tears. "Because when I came out to you, I was looking for support. I needed some sign my family wouldn't reject me, and all you've done since then is try to gaslight me."

Her heart pounded at a thousand beats per minute. She never spoke to her mother like this, but something inside her just... broke. Kyle's lower lip quivered. When she'd come out to Aunt Terry at the age of fifteen, the woman wrapped her into a huge hug, gave her a mug of her weird herbal tea, and said thank you. The response had meant everything and was so, so different from the Arctic inquisition she'd received from her parents.

"'Gaslight' seems a bit melodramatic," Mom said, refusing to acknowledge any sort of wrongdoing in the situation, like always.

Enough. Kyle had enough.

"Which is exactly what you're doing now, and I'm done with it. I'll see you at the Christmas party," Kyle said. "And after that, who knows. If you want to be a part of my life, you've got to do some major soul-searching." With that, she hung up on her mother.

For a moment, she stared at her phone, unable to process the way those bombs dropped on her confidence. She should be feeling strong, triumphant after standing up to her mother, but an incessant hollowness thumped in her chest. All the pushback confirmed was the truth she'd ignored for years—her parents would never be there for her.

Five minutes before, she'd been fine with this limbo with Chelsea, needing to spend the night with her even if the woman didn't want her in the long run. Even if she was a friend with benefits or the dirty secret.

Except those comments Mom made carved right into her chest until she bled.

Fake girlfriend. That's what she'd be bringing to the Walker Family Christmas, and the entire time would be an empty reminder she was never good enough for the real thing. Just like she'd never been the daughter her parents wanted either, and they kept trying to dance around it for years and years and years. The idea of her mother's critical expression or casual jabs grew unbearable—solely because of how bad she wanted the situation to be a reality. Kyle might be able to withstand the criticisms if she was coming home to vent in her girlfriend's arms.

But that had never been on the table. She'd allowed her fantasies to run away with her and stupidly got attached.

Heat prickled at her eyes again, and her nails bit crescent moons into her palm. Why did she ever think she could do this in the first place?

A knock sounded at her door, snapping her to the present. Her phone still sat in her hand, the reminder of the conversation pulsing in the air. Kyle swiped at her eyes, even though she hadn't shed any tears, as if she could hide the turmoil broiling through her.

She couldn't do this anymore. She'd already burned one bridge tonight, and the lit match was still in hand.

Kyle strode down her steps, numbness seeping through her veins and spreading from the pain radiating inside her chest. Her heart pounded hard, the boom, boom, boom of a bass drum. She brought the door open, and Chelsea strolled right in like she had a thousand times before.

"My fucking father," Chelsea exclaimed as she led the way up the steps. "He's taken it upon himself to invite Noah to Christmas, even though we're divorced."

Because you haven't told him. About us.

Kyle swallowed hard, following her up the steps. If anything, that just confirmed the fact she needed to put the brakes on here and now. She couldn't be the closeted fling, fake girlfriends, or anything else of the sort. She was proving her mother right at this point, and the truth pared away at what remained of her heart.

Her eyes stung again, but she summoned the nerve to tap Chelsea on the shoulder.

Chelsea spun around, and the moment her gaze landed on Kyle's face, her brows furrowed together. "What's wrong, sugar?"

Kyle sucked in a breath, steeling herself. She needed to do this. For her own sanity.

"The whole arrangement's off, Chels. The fake-girlfriend thing next week. I can't do it anymore—any of this. I thought I'd be okay with it, but I want a relationship. I want—" Her voice wavered, but she forged on regardless. "I want someone who's not afraid to be with me for real."

Chelsea opened her mouth to speak, but Kyle put her hand up. If she didn't get this out, she never would. "I know we made plans to hang out, but I need space right now. It's going to take me some time to readjust, to get my head on straight."

Kyle didn't lift her hands to escort her to the door, praying Chelsea would storm out on her own. That she'd hate her enough to never want to speak to her again and Kyle could shut her eyes and try to blank out the pain. Kyle still couldn't look up to see her expression, otherwise she might shatter. "I need you to go."

The words came out in a hoarse scrape, and she had to employ every ounce of resistance to keep the tears penned back.

When she brought her gaze to meet Chelsea's, the sight socked her in the gut. The woman's jaw dropped, and her umber eyes darkened as if she were devastated, lost. Pain radiated from her expression, raw, unrelenting pain like the exact sort Kyle felt. The sort that had her reaching forward like she could smooth out the creases.

Chelsea took a step back, the movement hitting like a slap to the face. "If that's what you need," she said, her voice chilling like ice. She'd never heard that tone from Chelsea, and she didn't want to ever again. It was like stepping into a frozen lake midwinter.

Chelsea pivoted on her heel and began to walk down the steps.

Kyle stood glued into place there with her hands balled into fists at her sides. She listened to the thump of Chelsea's footsteps and then the creak and thump as the door shut behind her.

For several minutes, all she could do was stand and stare. But eventually, the tremors overtook her entire body, traveling up her legs and her arms until she just shook and shook like she was standing on the icy streets outside with no jacket. She gritted her teeth together so hard her jaw might snap, but then she slipped, and once her jaw softened for a heartbeat, the prickle of heat behind her eyes unleashed.

Tears flowed freely down her cheeks, and her legs ceased to hold her up anymore as she sank to her knees. Kyle crumpled to the floor beneath her and clutched at the carpet. The sobs flowed out from her in wracking torrents, but she couldn't stop.

Chelsea had been the first ray of light she'd grasped onto in so, so long. The way she looked at her and how she encouraged her made Kyle believe this could be something more. In the time they'd spent together, she'd gotten more comfortable than she ever had with another soul, and she'd believed that meant something. But this far in, Chelsea remained silent. Kyle couldn't go on any longer.

She'd walked as far as she could, but her feet failed her.

For Chelsea, she'd been willing to risk her oldest friendship and what remained of her heart.

In the end, she'd lost all three.

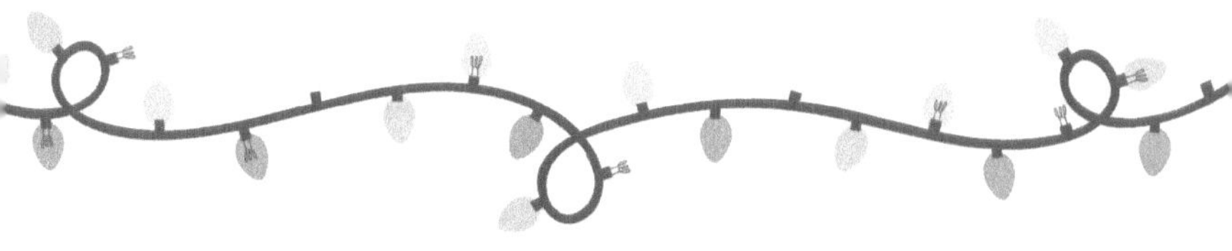

CHAPTER EIGHTEEN

Chelsea had spent almost every night this week at the bar.

The one real thing on her agenda for the weekend had been the Walker Christmas Party, but Kyle had cancelled the whole arrangement. Not only that, but she'd called it quits between them. Truthfully, Chelsea had herself to blame. All she'd needed to do was fucking speak up, but with all the pressures from her dad and the divorce, she'd let herself fall hard into the comfort Kyle offered.

Chelsea finished her first shiraz of the night, one of what she hoped would be many. She'd need the liquid courage—at least, if her sister decided to show up. Otherwise, she'd need to drown her sorrows in more alcohol because that always worked.

Julie, her waitress, wandered over with a fresh glass of wine, like an angel. It also didn't hurt that she'd been working here most of the time Chelsea had been coming in and could see she was going through a quarter-life crisis, or whatever this was.

Chelsea clutched the stem of the glass and stared into the deep red contents. The truth was, the ache in her chest ever since that night hurt far worse than her divorce. She'd missed the routine with Noah and simply having someone around, but with Kyle—she missed everything.

This didn't filter in like the brief, transitory sadness of looking into an empty room once filled with Noah's stuff. This hit her like she was sixteen at Pine Street Park after her first boyfriend dumped her, the guitarist in a punk band she swore she'd be with forever. She'd stumbled with blurred eyes over to her junker Chevy and sat in the passenger's seat, hot tears flowing down her cheeks. Over the years, she'd hidden those tears more and more, but the night Kyle sent her home, she'd vaulted right back to those teenage years when her heart was still open. Before she'd started hiding her softer sides from the world.

Part of her longed to call Kyle, to tell her everything, but her head was so fucked right now—would Ky be pissed at her for not respecting her space? The sole person who might know was the one she'd been avoiding since they'd gotten found out on Friendsgiving. Chelsea heaved out a long breath as she stared at the dark ceiling and the deep amber lights, wanting to find an answer somewhere, anywhere.

She caught movement from her periphery, and Chelsea glanced up in time to see Aubs saunter her way. Her sister looked determined, which she did most days, so she couldn't gauge if Aubs was angry, happy, relieved—fuck, anything.

Chelsea took another swig of her shiraz. Not like the alcohol settled her nerves. What did she have to lose at this point? Even if Kyle didn't want her any longer, she could never be the good kid in Dad's eyes again, not while she refused the way he kept trying to shove Noah back into her life. Maybe he just didn't want another of his daughters to catch the gay, because clearly, that was how it worked.

Aubs slid into the seat opposite her, her expression unreadable. "About damn time you talked to me."

Chelsea shrugged, staring into the depths of her drink. "You wanted answers I didn't have."

"No, I wanted to know what was going on in your head," Aubs said, stabbing her fingertip onto the table to make her point. Julie swung around for Aubrey's order, a rum and coke, of course, and made a quick exit, as if she also saw the storm clouds focused on the table between them.

"Look," Aubs said, spreading her palms on the table in front of her. "Back at Friendsgiving I was surprised, and I freaked out. You're not the one I'm pissed at here, Chels."

Chelsea's gaze snapped up to Aubrey. "And why would that be?"

Aubrey set her jaw, stubbornness rising to the surface like always. "Kyle's been my best friend for years, and she's been loyal as anything, at least until now. Not only did she keep what was going on between you secret the whole time, but hell, Chels, you were in a vulnerable place and she took advantage."

"She's not you, Aubs." The bitter words exploded from Chelsea's tongue before she could reign them in. Anger pulsed through her anew. She was enraged that her sister would treat Kyle that way after years and years of loyalty and gentleness. Kyle alone had been there for them during Mom's run-in with cancer, even when her own dumbass husband never showed. And last year, when Mom had another scare, Kyle rallied support for her back then too.

And that was before she'd ever gotten to know the woman on a close, personal level.

"Fuck you too, Chels," Aubrey spat, her dark eyes flashing with irritation. Not like they hadn't fought this way before—when she and Aubrey got into it, neither of them held back the sharpened knives.

"In the entirety of your friendship with her, has the woman ever possessed a predatory bone in her body?" Chelsea argued, refusing to let go of this one. She might've fucked things up with Kyle, but she couldn't stand if she'd ruined things between Kyle and Aubs too. When her sister didn't respond at first, her lips forming a thin line, Chelsea continued. "Who do you think initiated things between us? It sure as hell wasn't Kyle."

Aubs opened her mouth and shut it again, her brows drawing together as she processed the infor-mation. Chelsea leaned back in the seat and tapped the edge of her glass with her fingernail, the rest of the unspent rage simmering inside her. She loved her sister with all her heart, but sometimes Aubs just had her head stuck up her ass. It was a family trait.

"But you're not gay," Aubs said at last, her tone softer, a bit of her confusion leaking through.

Chelsea heaved out a sigh. "I might not be full-out lesbian, but I'm pretty sure at this point I'm bi. I started dating Noah and got married so early that I never got a chance to experiment or find myself." Chelsea took another sip from her shiraz. "And Kyle and I started hanging out as friends—both of us the single kids in the crew, so our schedules were wide open. Somewhere along the way, I realized she's fucking amazing, hot as hell, and I wanted to sleep with her."

Aubrey's face crinkled. "Oh, gross. Kyle's like a sister to me."

Chelsea bit back her amusement. "A sister who you're ignoring for no valid reason at all."

Aubrey tugged on the end of her ponytail, the gesture so familiar it hurt. As much as she'd kept Aubs at a distance, being able to talk with her sister like this offered comfort she'd be stupid to not grab ahold of.

"Fuck," Aubs said, glancing at her. The wince in her gaze was all the apology she'd ever needed. "I guess after the way I used to go for women fresh out of relationships...."

"You figured she was doing the same, forgetting that we both know Kyle's not the type," Chelsea finished for her. She should've realized why Aubs flipped like she did—her big sister had always been protective as hell over her.

Julie swung over with Aubrey's drink, and Aubrey lifted the glass up at once, gratefully taking a sip. "I'll make it right with her, I promise," Aubs said. She put the glass down but kept her palm wrapped around it.

"You better, Brea-gol," Chelsea teased, trying to lighten the mood.

Aubs lifted her middle fingers. "Thanks, Chelly. So, are the two of you dating now? Goddamn, that's weird."

Chelsea paled a little and tossed back more wine. This was the conversation she hadn't wanted to broach because everything felt so raw still, so close to the surface. "I fucked that one up. I...." Chelsea blew out a breath, trying to stave off the prickle beneath her skin and the tears threatening to rise to the surface again. "Kyle was nothing but patient with me, but I was too conflicted to ever make a claim as to what we were."

"Lived that damn life," Aubrey said, a half smile rising on her face. "I had to grovel with Selina after the way I refused to acknowledge shit. I didn't think you were like that, though—is the hesitance about Noah? The divorce?"

Chelsea shook her head, her lips forming a thin line. If she said the words, these tears would spill over, and she hated the weakness. She sucked in another breath.

Aubrey's gaze latched onto hers, darkening. "It's about Dad, isn't it?"

Chelsea's lower lip trembled, and she clutched the wine glass hard enough she thought the stem would snap. This wasn't the time or place to break down. Somehow, she managed to suck back enough oxygen to calm herself while Aubrey watched, surprisingly patient.

"You're worried he's going to start treating you like he's treated me all these years," Aubrey said, filling in the blanks. "God, I hate how the stubborn old fucker interferes. Baby girl, I've noticed the way you've tried to smooth things between us, how you've always stepped in line to minimize fights. You know that's not your job, right?"

Chelsea swallowed hard. "I love our family, Aubs. I don't want to lose it."

Aubrey shook her head. "You won't. You're allowed to have an opinion that doesn't line up with his. You're allowed to live your life the way you see fit. Look, Dad and I fight a lot, and sure, I hate how he gets about my 'lifestyle,' but has that ever stopped us from having a family Thanksgiving? Even if he's a dick sometimes, he's still my father, and he's willing to try to make things work in his own way. I'm just impatient, and he's slow as fuck."

Chelsea's lips turned up in a wavering smile. "You're not kidding. His idea of progress is only saying one prayer at family dinner."

Aubs reached across the table and squeezed Chelsea's hands together while looking her in the eyes. "You know you'll always have me, Chelly. And you know if you want to date a woman, even if it's my best friend, you've got my support. I didn't realize what was going on or where your headspace was at, and I'm sorry."

"Love you, sis," Chelsea murmured. She let out another heavy breath. "I fucked things up with Kyle, though. She told me she couldn't take it anymore and needed space."

Aubrey rolled her eyes and stared at the ceiling. "That's because my gumdrop button of a best friend has her own insecurities she's struggling with due to her asshole mother. Ky's not going to make the strong move here—that's never been her, and I should've realized the truth earlier. If she's who you want, you're going to need to stake your claim."

Chelsea nodded slowly. This week, she'd been wrapped up in the hopelessness of the situation, thinking she'd be stuck in this complicated misery forever. Everything reminded her of Kyle, from passing their brunch spot to any bakeries along the way, the stress-baking habit she found endearing. Even waking up in her own bed, she kept trying to latch onto the scent of Kyle in the sheets from the other night that had started with unforgettable sex and ended the following morning with pancakes.

For the first time, the first threads of resolve settled inside her. When she'd found the courage to leave Noah, she'd promised she wouldn't get stuck in limbo again, yet when she'd started to fall for Kyle, she landed back in the same pattern of not making a move, too afraid of drastic change.

Like she hadn't learned a damn thing.

Chelsea nodded. "She's the only one for me, Aubs. She makes me feel safe, loved—she makes me happy."

Aubs shook her head, a grin spreading on her

lips. "That's all I've ever wanted for you. So, screw Dad, screw Noah. Go get your girl back."

Chelsea's heart fluttered, and she grabbed onto the feeling with all her might. The road might be turbulent ahead, but she was ready to face it. "I've got a plan."

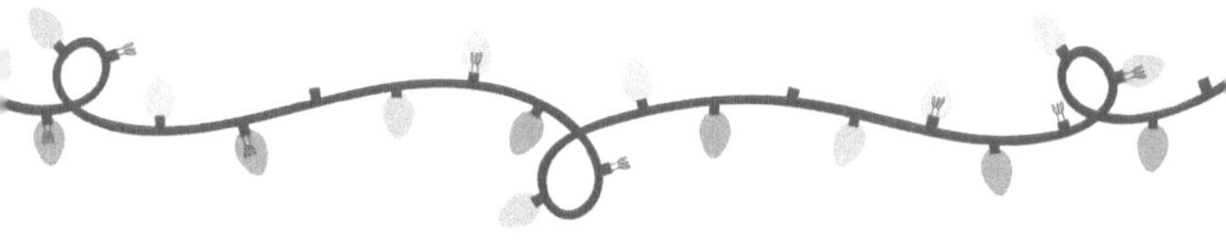

CHAPTER NINETEEN

WALKER FAMILY CHRISTMAS WAS TOMORROW, and Kyle couldn't be more miserable.

She'd glanced at her phone a thousand times a day ever since she'd pushed Chelsea away, some part of her hoping and wishing the woman might reach out regardless. But no, just like from her sister —silence.

Fuck, she missed Chelsea so damn much.

Her apartment felt emptier than it normally did. Chelsea filled up so many spaces whenever she came over, which had been all the time. In a short month, she'd gotten so used to having Chelsea around all the time, whether she dropped by to visit or they were going out together. A dozen and one times, she'd considered messaging her and calling a truce, claiming she didn't mean anything she'd said.

This loneliness was consuming, aching, and devastating.

This loneliness felt a lot like grief.

Yet she couldn't forget her mother's words if she tried. If she caved, then she'd never be able to rid herself of those fears—that she wasn't worth fighting for, that no one wanted her for a real relationship.

A knock pounded on her door. Ky's brows drew together as she nudged the blankets aside and pushed herself off from the slumped position on the couch she'd been in. She strode toward the steps, aware she looked a wreck. The moment she got home from work she'd thrown on pajama pants and cracked open a cider, needing to cocoon herself in the middle of some Netflix distractions.

As she reached for the knob, her heart sped in anticipation. There was only one person she longed to see standing on the other side, but she cursed herself for hoping.

Kyle tugged the door open.

Sky and Mia stood in the doorway, both looking sheepish. Kyle tried to maintain a solid expression so that her disappointment didn't leak through.

"Hey," Mia said, taking the first step inside. "I

know we should've called, but you've seemed down this week, so we took the initiative to visit."

Ky bobbed her head in a nod, unable to voice the words. Even though Aubs hadn't responded to any of her texts, she hadn't lost everyone, and that meant something. Still, Aubrey's absence hurt.

"If you're hoping for entertainment, though, I've got to warn you all I have is stale takeout pizza and a weird assortment of condiments in the fridge," Kyle said as she walked up the steps and back into her apartment.

"We're not total monsters, Ky," Sky teased as she followed behind her. "Mia and I brought some beer and cookies."

Kyle's heart squeezed tight. She'd been feeling so, so alone as of late, and she hadn't wanted to impose on Sky or Mia. Right then and there, she loved them all the more for showing up on her doorstep, even though she always took a little bit to adjust to surprises. "As long as this isn't an intervention or anything," she murmured.

"Why, do you need an intervention?" Sky asked. Mia placed the container of cookies on the coffee table and took a seat on the opposite couch while Sky plunked down beside her.

Ky shrugged, unable to come up with much of an

answer. "I'm just up to my usual shit, chasing after women who are never going to want me."

Sky lifted a brow as she nabbed a beer from the six pack. "If you're talking about Chelsea, she seemed to want you very much. Trust me, I noticed early on."

Kyle's smile strained. "Not enough to make any claims. Look, I don't want a fling or to be someone's dirty secret. I want a relationship, like what you guys have. What Aubs and Selina have." That truth grounded her when nothing else did. She'd been willing to be patient, but as much as her mom's words hurt, she'd come to understand she wasn't getting what she needed.

Kyle didn't want a bar hookup or a friends-with-benefits thing. She longed for what she'd almost had with Chelsea—getting to wake up with a partner in the mornings, cooking meals together, and cuddling on the couch after work.

Sky reached over and squeezed her knee. "That's what you deserve, Kyle. I'm not here to sound the alarm or invoke the Rehoboth Pact. Out of the three of us, you're the one who never needed it. You needed someone willing to fight for you."

"It's true," Mia joined in. "Aubs and Sky were the anti-commitment kids, and I'm grateful for the

Pact every day. But you're different, girlie. You're meant for commitment and long-lasting relationships. We've just been waiting for someone to see all the untapped potential inside you."

Kyle's eyes heated, and she gulped to chase her tears back. According to her mother, that day would never arrive.

A knock sounded at the door, followed by the rattle of the knob.

Kyle glanced over and then back at Sky and Mia. Both of them had hesitant grins on their lips. "We invited one more into the mix."

The steps creaked, and before Kyle could register, Aubs strode into the living room.

"Move over, Sky," Aubs said, stalking straight over to Kyle. Sky lifted a middle finger but scooched over on the couch.

A lump formed in Kyle's throat. After messaging her for the past few weeks, she'd given up hope that Aubrey would talk to her before Christmas, let alone at all. Aubrey plunked into the spot beside her and threw her arms around her in a bone-breaking hug. Kyle sank into it, tears welling in her eyes. She'd missed her best friend so damn much.

"I fucked up, and I'm sorry," Aubs murmured in her ear. "Chelsea set me straight."

A tear slid down her cheek, not just from having Aubrey here squeezing the breath from her, but at the idea that Chelsea still thought about her, that the woman might care.... She didn't know how it was possible to miss someone this much, but every thought of hers kept circling back to Chelsea Moore. She missed her enough to cave, enough to go back to whatever limbo they had going on—yet she knew the second those insecurities rose again, she'd bolt.

Aubs squeezed her again. "I fucking missed you, Ky."

"Missed you too," Ky murmured, burying her eyes in Aubrey's shoulder. A few sniffles came out that she tried to restrain. She was pretty sure she was leaving tear stains on Aubrey's shirt too.

Aubrey pulled back and clutched at her knees. "I had the whole situation backwards, and I focused so hard on talking to my sister first that I cut you out cold. That wasn't fair, because you've always been a sister too. Which makes it weird with the two of you being a thing."

Kyle shook her head, grief clawing at her chest anew. "Nah, we're not a thing anymore."

Aubrey shook her head and grabbed a beer. "I wouldn't write her off just yet."

Kyle snagged a beer to chase her cider with,

needing something more after this emotional over-load of a night. "I hope you're right" was all she managed in response, and Aubrey didn't volunteer anything else.

Aubrey glanced at Netflix. "You were watching *The Fellowship of the Ring* without us? Looks like you're only at the start of it."

Kyle shook her head, a hesitant grin spreading on her lips. "Well, excuse me for not realizing I'd have company."

"Eat a cookie," Mia called over. Sky pushed up and settled next to her on the couch. "I promise they're not poison. I'm pretty sure you can't fuck up chocolate chip, right?"

"Babe, you can definitely fuck up chocolate chip," Sky teased. "But I'll eat your damn cookies anyway."

Aubrey nudged Kyle in the knee, meeting her eyes. "We okay?" she mouthed.

Kyle nodded. As big as the blowup between them had been and how the silence in the interim stung, one of the things Kyle loved about Aubs was how the woman owned her mistakes. Even though part of her longed to ask what Aubrey's cryptic response about Chelsea meant, tonight she just wanted to be here with her best friends. She'd spent so much time worrying about the changes to their friend group, but when it mattered, they'd all come crawling out of the woodwork.

"We're still in the Shire, guys, so buckle up," Ky said, settling into the seat with her beer.

"Selina sends her love too. She's working tonight," Aubs said, kicking her feet up on the coffee table like she always did.

Kyle settled down in her couch and put the movie back on play. She couldn't help but glance around the room. Sky pretended to gag on one of Mia's cookies while Mia punched her in the arm, and Aubs sat beside her tipping back a beer, her gaze front and forward on the movie. Kyle's heart squeezed tight. She loved this crew with all her heart. Kyle grabbed her cozy blanket and took a sip from her beer, sinking into the movie.

She'd need every bit of tonight to get through tomorrow.

KYLE PULLED up in front of Aunt Terry's house, a two-story with cream siding, a black roof, and a rolling lawn. The woman hosted Walker Family Christmas every year and was one of the main reasons Kyle looked forward to this event. Dealing with her mother and father ranked lowest on the list of why she showed.

Except today would be awkward on the Aunt Terry front too, because last time they talked, she told her she'd be bringing her girlfriend, Chelsea. And she'd either have to explain that she'd recruited her friend to be a fake girlfriend, or that they'd broken up—both of which had gotten so muddled when they started sleeping together that she didn't know what story to go with.

She shut off her car engine, trying to ignore the sweat pricking her palms. Nerves rode her in a fierce way, a restlessness refusing to settle. Maybe she should've held out and waited before walking away from Chels. She always felt a thousand times better with Chelsea Moore at her side.

Except if she'd showed up with Chelsea as her fake girlfriend, every comment from her mom would have her dying a little more on the inside with every bit of disbelief that someone could choose her.

Kyle sucked in another sharp breath and snagged her container of cookies she'd baked for the event, this time chocolate with peanut butter chips. She hopped out of her car. Before she started striding down the walkway, she glanced up and down the line of cars, wanting to scope out who'd already arrived.

One car stopped her still.

The door creaked open, and Chelsea stepped out.

The mere sight of her knocked the breath from Kyle's chest. Chelsea wore a gray peacoat, but Kyle caught the crimson of a flared skirt beneath it, and the way she'd styled her long, cascading waves came together with the golden hoops in her ears to frame those heartbreaker features. Chelsea's dark eyes were lined in kohl and her sensual lips painted carmine. Honestly, she looked like she strode off the pages of Vogue.

Kyle sucked in a sharp breath of winter air, which prickled down her throat like broken glass. This was the one woman she'd been longing to see more than any other. Each day without Chelsea had stretched on longer than the last.

Chelsea strode in her direction, her gaze so intense that Kyle couldn't move from her spot.

Chelsea stopped in front of her, close enough to touch. There was a hesitance in her gaze, a flicker of fear. "Have a second to talk?"

"Yeah," she murmured, tilting her head toward the car. "Why don't we go somewhere warm. Unless you want my extended family members to get nosy and wonder what we're up to, because guaranteed, Aunt Betty's peering out the window."

"Can't have Aunt Betty interfering," Chelsea joked, even though her voice faltered.

Part of Kyle was tempted to just accept the fake-girlfriend thing, if only to have Chelsea in her life again. Yet the other part of her who'd taken a stand didn't want to travel backwards. Still, curiosity bubbled within her regardless.

The two of them crunched across the frozen grass in silence, and Kyle climbed back into her car, turning the engine on so the heat blasted through again. Chelsea slid in on the other side, the door closing with a click.

"How've you been?" Kyle asked, feeling like an idiot for the generic question that jumped out of her mouth.

"Fucking miserable without you," Chelsea said, that sharp honesty driving right into her heart.

Kyle swallowed hard. She'd been feeling the same, but she hadn't dared to believe Chelsea might be suffering too.

Showing up at her family Christmas shindig, though.... Did that mean something?

The hope thudded in her chest something fierce, even as she tried to give it a stern warning.

"Look, I thought about a thousand different ways to do this, and Aubs told me if I showed up at your house with a puppy and my shit in a moving van you might have a nervous breakdown, so I showed up here instead," Chelsea said. "But when it came down to the basics, this was the first promise I ever made you, and you're someone who values actions over words."

Kyle licked her lips. Chelsea wasn't wrong. She didn't react well with sudden change and hated showy displays, but proven loyalty had always meant the world. She kept her mouth shut and let Chelsea continue. The woman's brows drew together, and her gaze filled with pain. Chelsea reached between them to grab Kyle's hand, and in that instant, the touch connection meant everything.

"I'd been waiting," Chelsea burst out. "I wanted to tell you how I felt. I did, but I'd waited so long out of fear, and then I wanted to make it special, and.... Yeah."

Kyle waited, unable to ignore the rising thump, thump, thump in her chest, a thrill she didn't dare latch onto yet.

Chelsea stared at her, those dark eyes so

intense she couldn't look away if she tried. "I never meant to make you feel like you weren't worth chasing after, sugar. I never wanted to hurt you. When I started realizing my feelings for you, I had so much to sort through between my divorce, my situation with my dad, and coming to grips with the fact that I'm bisexual. And you were so damn patient."

Chelsea sucked in a shaky breath. "But I should've told you, Kyle Walker. Nothing about what was going on between us was fake. I don't know if I started falling for you the first morning I woke up in your bed hungover as hell when you took care of me and made me breakfast, or one of the countless nights I curled up on your couch with you. At some point, those feelings became terrifyingly real. And even though you've never voiced the way you felt, you've made it known all along—through your tenderness, your care, and those gorgeous hazel eyes that don't hide a damn thing."

Kyle's lower lip trembled as she tried to sort through the tidal wave of emotions cresting inside her. "Does that mean...." An exquisite pain unfurled in her chest. Chelsea Moore had been everything she'd ever wanted in a partner, in a person, and yet she never believed the woman would choose her.

That the woman would harbor a fraction of the intense feelings that stirred in Kyle's own chest.

"It means I love you," Chelsea said, her grip on Kyle's hand tightening. Her tone remained resolute in a world that was anything but, a gravitational force that Kyle swung toward again and again and again. "I love you, and I don't want to spend another day without you. This past week has been pure torture, and I just want you back in my life."

Heat welled in Kyle's eyes again as those words poured from Chelsea's lips, the very ones she'd been longing to hear. She could barely believe the woman had shown up here after Kyle had pushed her away. Even more, she could barely believe the words coming from her lips, the confession of a love she'd discounted as an unfulfilled fantasy a long time ago.

"You'll be my girlfriend?" Kyle managed to choke out, her voice thick. She clutched Chelsea's hand tighter with the question, that disbelief still ringing through the air.

Chelsea let out a watery laugh. "I'll be any damn thing you want me to be, sugar."

Some string inside Kyle snapped, the distance between them far too much. She leaned forward and grabbed Chelsea by the nape to close the space between them. Their lips crushed together, and the relief that flowed through Kyle at the connection was like walking into her warm apartment after a long, aching day at work to curl up in a blanket. Their kiss carried all of the sharp yearning that had burned within her for so long combined with the tenderness of their time together, every lazy caress and every sweet touch.

Chelsea's scent wrapped around her, the almond and leather she'd longed for, and a few tears pricked at her eyes. Their lips caressed each other's, and Chelsea took control of the kiss. Her tongue swept in with a claiming force that rendered Kyle helpless every time. She belonged with this woman. She belonged *to* this woman. Unbridled joy filtered through her veins, running rampant. After wanting for so long, she could barely process this reality.

They pulled back for air, their gasps echoing in the car.

Kyle met her gaze. "I love you, Chelsea Moore."

Chelsea offered a cocky grin, which wavered slightly. "I know. Now, I believe I've got a Christmas party to attend as your girlfriend."

Kyle swiped at the imprint Chelsea's lipstick made on her lips, cleaning up the edges. Giddiness swept through her, and she couldn't restrain her grin.

Chelsea's eyes danced, the same joy shining back in them.

"You sure you don't want to just head on back to my place?" Kyle asked, her eyes crinkling with how hard she smiled.

Chelsea licked her lips. "Now there's a tempting offer. But I made you a promise, and I refuse to let you weather your harpy of a mother alone. We're going to be obnoxious, and if I hear a damn criticism out of that woman's mouth, I might start a fist fight."

Kyle shook her head, the smile still just as wide. "Not necessary. I already told her off myself. I... realized I was letting too many people walk all over me, and I needed to take that stand."

Chelsea dragged her thumb across Kyle's jawline, the sensation sending a sinful tingle through her. "I hate that I was one of those people."

Kyle squeezed her hand again. "You're here now. That's what matters."

"And I'll be in your bed tonight," Chelsea responded, a wicked grin lighting up her features. "And the night after that, and the one after that. I might've waited to pack my entire place up, but I'll have you know that I already packed a box of my stuff that's sitting in my backseat—toothbrush, changes of clothes, and my Nintendo Switch. You know, in case this gamble went well. Just try getting rid of me now that we've gone all official."

"Never," Kyle said. "I'd never get rid of you, Chelsea Moore." Chelsea's eyes glistened the slightest bit, and Kyle's heart pumped harder. After all of the time Chelsea had spent at her apartment, Kyle couldn't wait to start having her stuff infiltrate. She loved the way the woman filled up the lonely spaces in her place. "I might've been startled by the puppy and moving truck, but Aubs was wrong on that front. For you? I'd welcome all that chaos into my life with open arms."

Chelsea leaned in to press her forehead against Kyle's, the motion so gentle and tender that it stroked something deep inside her. "You're making me want to take you right in this backseat, so we better get moving before I pounce."

Kyle reached down and gave her hand a squeeze. "Let's go face the family then. I can't wait for them to meet you."

For once, she meant it. She'd spent so much time worrying about this Walker Family Christmas, but now, those fears dissolved. With Chelsea by her side, she could face anything.

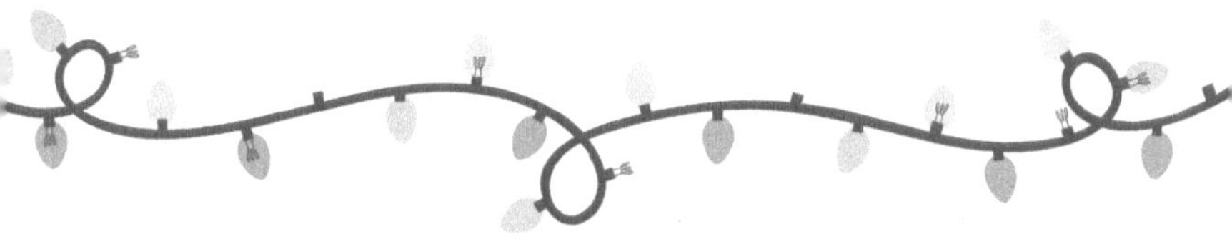

EPILOGUE
ONE YEAR LATER

Chelsea and Kyle stalked toward Aubs and Selina's townhouse for the Friendsmas shindig they were starting this year. Hopefully the tradition would catch. Chelsea reached down into the pocket of her peacoat until her fingertips settled on the small velvety box. Her throat was dry, even though she'd never been surer about anything in her entire life.

The past year with Kyle had been a goddamn dream. She'd come out to her dad by bringing Kyle to Christmas, and when he tried to get stony with her, Mom and Aubs dove in to defend. Things weren't the same between them, but they hadn't been ever since he tried to pull the underhanded shit with Noah. Through it all, Kyle had been there, a steadfast hand to hold, someone to curl up with at night, and whenever the mood struck, a willing submissive in the bedroom, an area they'd continued to explore more and more.

The second her lease went up, she moved in with Kyle, eager to leave the shitty memories behind. Philly was a fun city to live in, and she still saw the family plenty enough to keep them happy. Aubs had turned into their most steadfast supporter, soon realizing that with Kyle and Chelsea dating, she got all the family and bestie time she'd ever wanted.

When they neared the front door, Chelsea tugged Kyle's hand, signaling for her to stop.

Showtime.

Her heart thumped so hard it crept into her throat. Kyle turned around, casting her a curious look. When Chelsea sank to one knee, those hazel eyes grew even bigger. The chill from the concrete stoop seeped in past the fabric of her leggings, but inside, she burned. Chelsea tugged out the small black box and cracked it open to reveal the ring nestled inside.

She'd mulled over about a thousand things she wanted to say, eloquent speeches that never seemed like enough to describe the way this woman made her pulse pound and just how deeply she'd fallen in love. So all she said when she looked up was "You're worth forever, sugar."

Kyle's hand covered her mouth, and her eyes glossed over. A few shuddering sobs shook through her before she crouched in front of Chelsea, placing her hands on her knees.

She bobbed her head in a nod, a few stray tears streaking down her face.

Chelsea's lips curled into a grin, unable to help the surge of joy that burst through her veins right now, like pure, distilled sunrise. "Use your words, gorgeous."

"Yes," Kyle forced out, her grin watery as she leaned forward to tip her forehead against Chelsea's. "You're the only one I want, for life."

It was Kyle's tenderness, the effortless sweetness that made Chelsea fall. Kyle showed her love through every action, every time she went to bed early because Chelsea did, or every time she worked on her shoulders or stroked her hair after a rough day. Their home smelled like sugar and cinnamon, and the warmth didn't just coat Chelsea's skin, it seeped down into her pores until it filled her up from the inside out.

Chelsea popped the rose-gold ring out of the container, a small diamond in the center and brushed leaves along the side that she hoped Kyle would love. She slipped the band onto Kyle's finger and then stole one hell of a kiss from her woman. Their lips crushed together, and despite the wintry air surrounding them, she'd never felt warmer.

Her first marriage was one she'd tumbled into, but this one—this one, she chose.

Chelsea interlaced her fingers with Kyle's, breaking away from the kiss. "We should probably head in. Everyone's going to get impatient."

"Everyone...?" Kyle trailed off. Before she could piece her plan together, Chelsea rose, tugging Kyle up with her. She didn't bother knocking as she turned the knob and stepped inside Aubrey's house.

The whole crew waited in the foyer, from their friends, Sky, Mia, Aubs, and Selina, to her mom and dad, as well as Kyle's aunt Terry and her brother Jake. With the asshole way Kyle's mother and father treated the both of them, they hadn't been invited to the soiree. She refused to let her fiancée be the horrible woman's punching bag any longer.

"So," Aubs spoke up, breaking the silence. "What did she say?"

Kyle lifted her hand with the ring on it. Aubs punched the air, releasing a whoop, and the rest of the folks let out mingled cheers and hollers. Aubs threw her arms around Kyle, squeezing hard, and then passed her off to the rest who offered their congratulations. Chelsea tugged her sister into a hug next.

"Like you had any doubts," Chelsea murmured as she pulled back.

"Not in the slightest," Aubs said with a grin, shaking her head. "I've never seen Ky this happy with anyone. Though you're making me look bad, Ms. Marriage Junkie."

Chelsea snorted. "I've heard Selina's rants on how you need three years to gauge a relationship. If you tried that shit early, she'd smack you in the head."

"My girl's overly cautious; what can I say?" Aubs responded, an affectionate look in her eyes as she glanced over at Selina.

Chelsea squeezed Aubrey's shoulder. "Let me go catch up with Mom and Dad."

"Good luck," Aubs said. They both knew she meant with Dad, not Mom.

Chelsea sucked in a breath and, on her way over, drifted her fingers across Kyle's back. The woman pulled away from her Aunt Terry, who was gushing. She beamed, a grin emanating out of those beautiful hazel eyes. Fuck, Chelsea was just as smitten as she was on that first day. Kyle tilted her head to the side, casting a questioning look in the direction of her parents.

"I've got this," Chelsea murmured, brushing her lips against Kyle's cheek. She nuzzled into the touch, and Chelsea resisted the urge to drag the woman somewhere private and kiss the hell out of her before she stripped her down to explore her body. Who knew engagements would be such a turn-on? She nipped at Kyle's earlobe, the ensuing flush well worth it, before she headed over to the opposite side of the room where her parents waited.

"Congratulations!" Mom threw her arms around Chelsea, squeezing her with an Aubrey-level hug. "We love Kyle, and I think the two of you will be perfect together."

Chelsea sank into her mom's embrace, so relieved at the eager acceptance that it almost made up for her father's silence. When Mom pulled away, Chelsea stood before her father. She knew he wasn't the type for big squishy hugs, but he stared at her with visible discomfort.

"Congratulations, *mija*," he said. He stuck his hands in his pockets and looked sheepish for a moment. "Your mother and I are happy for you." Even though he didn't meet her eyes, she could tell he was trying. In the strict environment her father had been raised, this might always be something he struggled with, but over the past year with both of his daughters bringing home their girlfriends—he'd made an attempt. And that's all she could ask for.

"Thanks, Dad," Chelsea said, stepping in to wrap her arms around him. A moment later, he hugged her back, and she sank into the embrace. Their relationship had changed, but Chelsea had learned that was okay too.

She pulled away and scanned around the room for her fiancée. Fuck, she loved that word. Kyle had been pulled away by Sky, Selina, and Mia this time. The four of them all laughed together, pure elation on everyone's faces. Chelsea had been absorbed into their friend group in a heartbeat and couldn't be happier. She'd even joined them on the yearly Rehoboth trip over the past year, enjoying the beach and the bars with her girlfriend.

Chelsea stepped up behind Kyle and wrapped her arms around her. Kyle leaned back, sinking into the embrace. She drew in the scent of brown sugar and cinnamon—her woman smelled like pure sweetness and the hearth. She smelled like home. Chelsea squeezed her a little tighter, never wanting to let go.

"Gross, guys. Get a room," Sky teased. Selina

smirked beside her as Aubrey launched herself into the mix.

"Hey, thank you," Kyle murmured, casting a vulnerable glance to Chelsea.

"For what?" Chelsea asked, her brows drawing together.

"For being you," Kyle responded, love shining clear in her eyes. "For seeing me, the real me, and choosing to fight. For being the first partner to make me feel like I matter."

Chelsea's throat tightened. Damn, she loved this woman. Every time she thought she couldn't fall deeper for her, she did. She tapped Kyle's ring with her fingernail, making a clicking sound. "That's a promise, because I'm not going to stop."

Even amid all of the chatter from friends and family, the bright smiles, the warm laughs, for a moment, the two of them were the only ones who existed in the room.

Chelsea brushed her lips against Kyle's cheek again, unable to help herself. "We're in this together, sugar."

Kyle nodded, her gaze shining as she looked back at Chelsea. In an instant, she got a brief glimpse of a future filled with more of this—of loving glances, of shared burdens, of days and nights with the one person on the planet who made her feel whole.

Kyle squeezed her arm tight, as if she saw the same future broadcasted out over the horizon, like the first glimpse of sunrise peering through the clouds.

"Forever."

LOOKING FOR MORE F/F romances and not yet read book one? Pick up **CONFINED DESIRES** today! Plus check out Katherine's M/M romance **MIDNIGHT HEIST**.

ACKNOWLEDGMENTS

This entire series was a pure joy to write, a light in the middle of the dark time during the pandemic while I was on furlough and pregnant. The warmth and friendship of the girls of this trilogy lifted me up and kept me sane, and I'm so thrilled to finally share them all with you. Cate, Landra, Amy, and Jenn were instrumental in this book, offering valuable insight on Kyle and Chelsea, and the story wouldn't be the same without their help.

The Rehoboth Pact Trilogy never would have flourished without the amazing team at Hot Tree Publishing taking a chance on these stories, and I'm forever grateful for their support and insight!

ABOUT THE AUTHOR

Katherine McIntyre is a feisty chick with a big attitude despite her short stature. She writes stories featuring snarky women, ragtag crews, and men with bad attitudes—and there's an equally high chance for a passionate speech thrown into the mix. As an eternal geek and tomboy who's always stepped to her own beat, she's made it her mission to write stories that represent the broad spectrum of people out there, from different cultures and races to all varieties of men and women.

Website: http://www.katherine-mcintyre.com
Newsletter sign-up: http://eepurl.com/duIScb

ABOUT THE PUBLISHER

Hot Tree Publishing opened its doors in 2015 with an aspiration to bring quality fiction to the world of readers. With the initial focus on romance and a wide spread of romance subgenres, Hot Tree Publishing has since opened their first imprint, Tangled Tree Publishing, specializing in crime, mystery, suspense, and thriller.

Firmly seated in the industry as a leading editing provider to independent authors and small publishing houses, Hot Tree Publishing is the sister company to Hot Tree Editing, founded in 2012. Having established in-house editing and promotions, plus having a well-respected market presence, Hot Tree Publishing endeavors to be a leader in bringing quality stories to the world of readers.

Interested in discovering more amazing reads brought to you by Hot Tree Publishing? Head over to the website for information:

www.hottreepublishing.com

www.ingramcontent.com/pod-product-compliance
Lightning Source LLC
Chambersburg PA
CBHW060804190726
48285CB00002B/536